A Candlelight Ecstasy Romance®

"I HAVEN'T MISSED A MAN," SHE SAID DELIBERATELY.

"If you think because I'm living alone that I'm some sex-starved, frustrated little . . ."

"Bronwyn, I didn't say that at all, and I didn't mean that." He was impatient again.

"You're implying that." So quickly he had stolen a certain power over her . . . and she resented it. "You don't know me at all, and I already have everything that I really need—"

"Bull." The growl was low-keyed, tinged with laughter.

A CANDLELIGHT ECSTASY ROMANCE ®

STORMY
SURRENDER

Jessica Massey

A CANDLELIGHT ECSTASY ROMANCE ®

Published by
Dell Publishing Co., Inc.
1 Dag Hammarskjold Plaza
New York, New York 10017

ISBN: 0-440-18340-5

Printed in the United States of America
First printing—March 1984

To Our Readers:

We have been delighted with your enthusiastic response to Candlelight Ecstasy Romances®, and we thank you for the interest you have shown in this exciting series.

In the upcoming months we will continue to present the distinctive sensuous love stories you have come to expect only from Ecstasy. We look forward to bringing you many more books from your favorite authors and also the very finest work from new authors of contemporary romantic fiction.

As always, we are striving to present the unique, absorbing love stories that you enjoy most—books that are more than ordinary romance.

Your suggestions and comments are always welcome. Please write to us at the address below.

Sincerely,

The Editors
Candlelight Romances
1 Dag Hammarskjold Plaza
New York, New York 10017

CHAPTER ONE

Bronwyn's eyes lazily fluttered open, then shuttered closed against the glare of midafternoon sun. The short, drugging nap felt just a little too good to wake up from; the morning had begun at five. She'd had a paintbrush in her hand since that hour.

Sleepily she roused just enough to turn on her back. Immediately the sun assaulted the cooler skin of her breasts and abdomen, soaking in both warmth and lethargy. Will-o'-the-wisp images floated in her mind. . . . Lorrie, a sweet rush of the softest memories, and Bronwyn thought fleetingly that the sun really had managed to heal. Just as the last six months of sun had toasted her skin to a rich dark gold, so it had sealed out some of the anguish from the winter before. She never thought it would happen. That she would feel again. That she would even want to.

For a few minutes she savored that awareness of everything around her, as if feeling were something new that she'd just discovered. Grains of sand tickled at her back; she could hear the surf fifty yards from her feet. A thousand things. The way a bead of moisture had collected in her navel, the way her toes were encrusted with sand, the way her long, sleek stretch of legs felt glowing in the heat. The two triangles of black bikini didn't deprive the sun of much territory. Even her hair, coal dark and shoulder length, had absorbed that penetrating heat, and she stretched languidly, conscious of the look and feel of her own body as she hadn't been in months.

Perhaps that was partly because of the dream. She had dreamed of Joe, and he had loved her dramatic looks, had valued her classic features and high-breasted slimness. That she was twenty-eight and had borne a child showed neither in her face nor her figure. Only when her huge brown eyes opened could one glimpse a haunting sadness, a woman's experience with life. But, then, Joe was not one to waste time on a woman's eyes.

In the dream it had been the day after Lorrie's funeral again, the day she had told him she wanted the divorce. She saw his face, as drawn and ashen with grief as her own. He hadn't wanted it. There would have been no divorce if she had given him a choice: no-fault was no scandal; his adulteries would have been. And she was the one who had really had no choice, but knowing that didn't lessen the guilt she still felt burdened with from time to time. She had never been cruel to another living soul. Only with Joe, and only that day.

Her eyes blinked open and she sat up, suddenly unbearably hot and restless. The dream was over, the past relegated where it had to be, to the realm of things that could no longer be changed, that had to be accepted and lived with.

The moment she moved, Gypsy lumbered over to her side, and a welcoming smile touched her lips. The big black Newfoundland woofed, pleased she was awake, impatient for their late afternoon swim. A cold wet nose nudged at her stomach and she chuckled, using both hands to tussle the big lug into obedience. Gypsy was her lifeguard. Currents had no respect for the best of swimmers, and her cottage bordered the windswept shores of the peninsula they called Merritt Island. Bronwyn had chosen that isolation, but Gypsy made that just a little easier. Not only was the breed 140 pounds of protection

10

and natural lifesaving instincts, but the pup's love of the water matched her own.

The dog lurched up and paced to the surf, then looked back at her. She could hardly fail to get the message. The tail was practically wagging back and forth at the speed of sound. She stood up with a lazy, sensual stretch, still trying to shake off the last waves of sleep, and, perhaps, the disturbing memories of the dream.

She noticed no one around and hadn't really expected to. The Atlantic coast could be threatening in October; the season brought with it a certain volatile pressure day by day that inhibited the casual vacationer, even for the neighboring New Smyrna. October's sun was mercurial, one minute hell-hot and the next gone, a storm threatening.

Waves pounded on the Florida sand, spitting out shells and crabs and seaweed indiscriminately, then going back to the depths for another load. The churning froth hit at Bronwyn's ankles, stinging just a little from the force of the tiny sharp shells. The next wave hit her sunwarmed thighs, and then it was easier beyond the first pulse of shore waves. The water rose and fell, a teasing lover beneath her scrap of black bikini, and as if for a lover, her nipples hardened and tightened when the water reached breast height. The slow torture was too much; she dove into the next wave, emerging with a gasp for its chill.

She heard Gypsy's sudden bark behind her, but paid no attention. There was a wait just beyond the sandbar, the wait for a wave with a long, powerful crest. One wave passed, and then another that she leaped for, none of them right. The third she watched come almost from the horizon, knowing it was right, knowing she could body-surf the entire way to shore on its power. She waited, and was half turned for the curl when she glimpsed the child.

The little redhead shrieked in the shallows, the lone sole in sight on the deserted beach, far too young to be alone at any time, and especially this day—the undertow strong enough to threaten the best of swimmers. With a sick sense of horror Bronwyn suddenly had the image of another child in front of her eyes—an illusion of blond hair and the same childish tummy; she even heard the same squeal of pleasure Lorrie had made a thousand times when a wave splashed.

Instincts overpowered emotions. She dove with the wave, her arms straining to gain distance by using the ocean's own force and momentum. Gasping for breath, she emerged in the shallows, fighting the strain of undertow on her legs as she searched for the child's face again. But there was nothing, no bob of a head, no bright lime swimsuit, just Gypsy, wagging her tail as Bronwyn neared. She closed her eyes, nauseated, sickeningly aware that the child must have been a hallucination. Gypsy would hardly be playing if there had been a child in trouble. It was all in her mind; the sick sense of loss she thought conquered in the last six months echoed inside like a feverish ache.

Suddenly she saw a man running in her direction, just an instant's glimpse of bronze skin and muscled leanness and shaggy, jet-black hair. He shouted something. Confused again, she half turned, heard Gypsy's sudden yelp, and saw the look of the dog, sleek and huge, already breaking through the surf. From nearly as far back as the wave she'd rode in, there was a sudden streak of lime, a choking cry.

She surged back in the water and dove, eyes burning, adrenaline and desperation streaking through her bloodstream. From behind her she was conscious of the man; from ahead she saw Gypsy's head bob up, go down again. Then she went down and under with a single prayer for speed.

Gypsy had already reached the child when she had surfaced. Tiny hands were digging around the big dog's

12

neck; the dog was furiously trying to tread water, patiently and repeatedly nudging the child's head above the surface with the instinct and years of intensive training. The girl was saved, but she didn't know it. Such frantic, gasping sobs . . . Bronwyn grasped her, unclenching the child's fingers from Gypsy's neck, putting the little fingers around her own. The child fought with an out-of-control desperation, her nails like razors and her kicks frenzied. Bronwyn stood so the waves could not crest in the child's face, cradling her, willing her own relief and calm to spirit into the child. Bronwyn's arms tightened, her voice soothing as she gained back her own breath, barely aware of the scratches and bruises the child had inflicted.

"Carroll!"

A cold palm touched her shoulder and the child's at the same time. The child wrenched from Bronwyn with a choking cry for her father; for just an instant Bronwyn felt an unbearable chill as the child's body was stolen from her. She felt the man's eyes on her, grateful, brooding, blue, and then his attention was all for the child.

He lost no time getting her to shore. Bronwyn could just glimpse the shaggy wet hair above her father's shoulders; his arms sheltered the rest of her. Those shoulders were broad for a man not overly tall, less than six feet by an inch or two, perhaps, but the body radiated power and strength. Every muscle moved as he walked; every part of his body was used in movement with a grace that was more supple animal than man . . . or, perhaps, in another arena, distinctly man.

She was just behind him as he laid the child on warm sand. He turned the girl to her stomach as he crouched down, his powerful hands rubbing the too-chilled little body. The child spit out salt water and started crying again. Gypsy hovered a few yards distant, whimpering every time the child did, and Bronwyn paused long enough to stroke appreciation to the dog for her help.

13

"Daddy . . . that water kept pulling me!" sobbed the child.

"I know, I know," soothed the man softly. "But it's all over now, Caro. Nothing's going to hurt you now. Nothing."

Bronwyn hurried for her beach towel and brought it back to them. He saw the towel, she knew that, but he was having a hard time keeping his hands anywhere but directly on his child. A measure of love so great, that for those few seconds he didn't even want the towel separating them, not a sign that he didn't realize the child needed immediate care. Bronwyn understood, and for the first time in those frantic minutes felt an unwelcome blur of tears in her eyes.

The man kept talking, smoothing back his child's tousled hair as the last of the wretching finally stopped. He swaddled her in the towel then, gently lifting her as he got to his feet. "Of course you were scared, Caro, of course you were . . ."

He had Bronwyn almost mesmerized with that deep, husky voice, the blend of tenderness and strength so uniquely male. Belatedly she rushed to her feet when he glanced distractedly back at her. "If you're closer . . . it's better than a half mile back to my place."

"Of course," she said swiftly, motioning to the wooden steps that bridged the breakwall to her yard. It was perhaps a hundred-yard walk, no more. Her mind, as his, was still totally immersed in the child, yet, fleetingly, she could not help but be aware that it was going to be the first time in a long time that she had allowed anyone anywhere near her private sanctuary. Not that it mattered. Nothing mattered but seeing that child warm and safe again.

"I just want to get her warm and dry as quickly as possible—"

"Of course," she said shortly, aching to snatch the child directly from his arms. He was wonderful with her; it was

14

just that the child's near brush with death reminded her too much of her own loss, and she craved to do the holding herself instead of just watching.

"Look. I can't thank you enough—"

"Bronwyn's the name. And don't be ridiculous!"

Gypsy scampered up the beach ahead of them, leading the way. Bronwyn trailed just a little; he had long swift strides and her own legs seemed to have just decided to be shaky. Reaction was setting in; her heart wouldn't stop pounding.

The beach stretched out on both sides of them, empty. To the south was Merritt Island, a wildlife sanctuary with its tufts of green spiky brush mounded above the sand, hiding its wealth of colorful lagoons and life-filled swamps. A half mile north was New Smyrna and its peppering of expensive condominiums—where the two must have come from. Her cottage was one of the last structures before the wild, deserted miles of Merritt.

Past the stairs, the man took the stone steps of the walk; Bronwyn spurted ahead of him by stepping into the stiff grass. If the blades were like needles under her feet, she didn't feel them. "Gypsy, stay," she called back to the dog as she opened the sliding glass doors and felt a rush of chilled air greet them. She hurried to flick off the thermostat completely, opening the doors wide to even the temperature as she motioned the two in behind her.

"If you'll let me take her," she offered, "I'll get her into a warm bath. The faster we get her warm the better, and then I think something to calm her stomach."

"I'd better do it. I'm afraid she's not going to let go of me."

Nonsense, Bronwyn thought privately, feeling a woman's instinct that she could get the child warmed and soothed down faster than any man, even the child's own father. But she flashed him an understanding smile as she led the way to the bathroom. A vise was not going to pry

15

that child away from him. In his shoes she would have reacted exactly the same.

She bent down to close the drain and start flooding warm water into the tub, brushing her hair back distractedly as she turned back up to him. "I haven't even asked your name."

"Austin. Steele."

She stood back up, waiting for the tub to fill. Her mind kept repeating that name; it suited him. It should have felt uncomfortable for the three of them to be standing in that little bathroom; for some crazy reason, it didn't.

"She hurt you," he said suddenly.

Bronwyn glanced down absently. The bikini top. One strap seemed to have ripped when the child had grasped so frantically in the water. There were scratches, even one ragged line with a drop of blood. Next to the child's safety they were nothing; she hadn't even noticed at the time. She glanced back up to tell him, and then somehow didn't.

Their eyes met. Physical awareness coursed through her at the look in his eyes, a rush of chemistry that shouldn't have existed, not at this place and time. And it wasn't that the suit was any less modest than any other bikini; the lost strap made no difference. But she was suddenly aware that the coolness of the house had firmed the supple shape of her breasts, that the nipples showed clearly through the damp fabric.

For two seconds they stared at each other. The child was on both their minds; it wasn't long. Long enough for her to memorize those magnetic eyes of his, their volatile, penetrating blue. The tan swimming trunks contrasted to a torso not only lean, but gunmetal hard. The face was long, with high cheekbones and an aquiline nose, and none of the roundfaced beauty of his daughter. *Raw* was the word that came to mind. Raw in look and raw in sexuality, the kind of man who knew exactly what he wanted in life and took it. And she couldn't remember a time in her life

16

when any man had looked at her exactly that way. . . .

"Bronwyn?"

Of course. The only reason he had stepped forward was because the tub was filled and she was in the way. Another emotion rose from the deep freeze of the last six months. Anger at herself. Of all the selfish, perfectly stupid . . . Swiftly she stepped around him, thinking to grab up fresh towels for when the child came out.

The child shuddered violently as Austin leaned over the side of the tub, cradling his daughter down in the water. Her little fingers clutched for his shoulders. "Just for a few minutes, Caro," he soothed her. "Just to get you warm, love. Everything's fine now, Caro."

It occurred to her later that she could well have left them then. Instead she knelt down at the opposite end of the tub, savoring the return of natural color and warmth to the child's body. Gradually her shaking stopped, and gradually two soft dark eyes ventured out from the crook of her father's shoulder where they'd been hiding. Bronwyn smiled at her reassuringly.

"I'm Bronwyn," she said very slowly. "That was my big black dog you saw in the water. Her name is Gypsy and she absolutely adores little girls. And I happen to have a special treat just for redheaded little girls with beautiful eyes like yours. Camomile tea. Have you ever heard of it?"

The child shook her head hesitantly, but her hold on her father's shoulders was gradually relaxing.

"It tastes like apples. Have you ever heard of a tea that tasted like apples?" She had the huge towel ready like a blanket as Austin lifted the child from the tub. "And we'll put lots of honey in it. You can sit right on your daddy's lap while you're drinking that. I might even make some for him if he's a very good boy."

The child responded with a little giggle, what Bronwyn had been hoping for. She couldn't stop herself from swiftly

17

kissing the child's cheek in reward, then her eyes rose swiftly to the hint of suggestive laughter in her father's. Trying to fit the epithet "good boy" on that tall virile form would be like trying to fit a halo on the devil.

CHAPTER TWO

"You decorated the place yourself, didn't you?"

"Yes." Bronwyn was in the kitchen, pouring boiling water over a blend of herbs in a cup for Carroll. She glanced up absently when Austin spoke, though her hand kept stirring.

The late afternoon sun streamed in the open balcony; pale coral drapes stirred at the windows. The room was huge and long and the furnishings were all coral or natural rattan, the living area divided by a counter from the kitchen. Everywhere there was light, Bronwyn had pots of the herbs she liked: camomile, rosemary, comfrey and sage, ginger and marigold. The pale greens were reflected in the kitchen colors, and the blend was serene and feminine to her own eye. She wondered vaguely how Austin saw it. Seated in a chair with Carroll on his lap, he was glancing at the painting above the coral couch.

Her own work rarely pleased her. Her art teachers used to tell her she was excellent with color and "feeling," but these days it was perfection in form she strived for—and rarely achieved. Still, she'd grown attached to that particular whimsical trio of sandpipers, a scene on the beach, done with long bold strokes of the brush gentled by muted corals, golds, and browns. In the corner was a very small, equally whimsical *B.* "Yours?" he questioned.

She ducked around the side of the kitchen. Holding steady the knot of her towel at her breasts, she carried the warm cup to the child. "It won't hurt her," she assured Austin. "It should just settle her stomach."

He nodded, taking the cup from her hands, but there was the barest slash of a smile for the avoided answer. Even as he was scooting Carroll up to a sitting position, she could feel a lightning bolt skim over her bare brown legs where the towel parted. God in heaven, those eyes . . . A blind man could see all his real concentration was on his child. It was just those quick penetrating flashes, as if a single study of her cottage yielded him a dozen conclusions, as if the quick brush of his eyes on her body yielded him more than conclusions.

Sexual vibrations were cheerfully humming along her nerve endings. She just didn't quite know what to do about them, how to turn them off. It just wasn't possible to treat him with the distance of a total stranger, not after what they had just shared. In that crisis she felt that she'd gotten to know almost unwillingly the kinds of things that mattered about him, and she found herself absently studying him while Carroll sipped her tea.

Tiny lines fanned out around his eyes and a spray of silver streaked his temples. There was just a touch of arrogance in the set of his chin. She had the feeling he'd taken on his share of comers, wearing his pride like a shield, and that he hadn't won every battle, just the ones that mattered to him. The aura was of strength and perception, cloaked in a man who valued his privacy. She felt both drawn and repelled. Mostly drawn, if she wanted to be honest with herself. The tenderness he showed his daughter touched her. But the evocative sexual vibrations he sent out disturbed her, knowing the daughter indicated a wife.

The child offered a shy sleepy smile of approval for the tea. "Would you like a little more?" Bronwyn coaxed.

She shook her head and Bronwyn turned to Austin. "You probably want to call her mother. I'm afraid I don't have a phone, but there's a man in the next cottage down—"

Again, too alert eyes met hers. "How could you not have a phone?"

"I just don't normally need one," she answered, and smiled again at his daughter, deliberately avoiding eye contact this time. "I'll be right back, sweetheart, if you change your mind about another cup of tea."

In a very few seconds the door was closed to her bedroom, the towel and bikini puddled on the floor, and a simple ivory shift pulled over her head. She snatched up a brush, pulling it through her tangled hair. The crisis was over, and any lingering state of nerves was undoubtedly due to standing around half naked. Yet she couldn't seem to conquer a disturbed feeling, a disorientation totally alien to the serene and settled Bronwyn who had emerged over the last six months. There was no excuse for it. He was obviously married and she couldn't have been less interested in a relationship. The only people she'd even talked to in the last six months had been grocers and shopkeepers; no one had been invited to invade the sheltered privacy of her cottage—because she wanted no one.

Less than five minutes later she came out of the bedroom, and already the child had fallen asleep on her father's lap. She studied Carroll's pink cheeks and half smile, the velvet mat of lashes sweeping a face that radiated contentment. "Please don't wake her, Austin," Bronwyn murmured. "I'm sure you're in a hurry to get her home, but she could nap in my room. . . ." She hesitated, adding a little wryly, "At least *I* would feel a whole lot better if I knew she was absolutely all right when she wakes up."

His smile held no hesitation. "All right," he agreed quietly, "but I do have to call Mary. She's the baby-sitter Caro got away from. Normally the two get on like a matched set—until the subject of water comes up, and

21

then they run in opposite directions." He cradled his daughter in his arms as he stood up. "You said you had a neighbor with a phone?"

She whispered the directions as he lay the child on the smooth apricot sheets. Carroll did not so much as stir. Austin glanced around the room, just once, and back at Bronwyn.

It was a huge room, too, with stark white carpeting and a background color of apricot. There were no furnishings except the bed and a small bedside table. The closet contained built-in drawers; there was no need for other furniture for the life she had been living. Simplicity served and the only time she was in the room was to sleep, but the bed stood, huge and alone, in that space.

"You live alone?" he questioned her quietly.

She nodded. "Yes. For the last six months."

"That's damned hard to believe of you, brown eyes." His eyes locked with hers just for that instant before he left the house to make his telephone call.

Irritably she let out her breath the moment he was gone. After checking one more time on Carroll, she made her way to the kitchen, leaving the bedroom door open.

It had been hours since she'd eaten. One of the joys of cooking solely for herself was being free to prepare exactly what she liked. After slicing a honey-baked ham, she prepared fresh mushrooms to sauté in soy sauce. She carried a sponge cake smothered in marshmallow frosting to the dining room table, then poured two glasses of wine and left one sitting on the counter. Vegetables—she liked peas, fresh and uncooked from the pod—perhaps a developed taste, she thought wryly, because Joe had liked them so overcooked they were mush.

When the dinner preparations were done, she stepped out on the terrace. At the corner of the house was a makeshift shower; she'd barely flipped on the faucets before Gypsy was beneath it, shaking off the sand and salt,

22

lapping her big pink tongue up for the cool spray. "Now dry off before you come in," Bronwyn instructed her firmly.

The dog gave her a reproachful look. Bronwyn grinned, and then impulsively leaned over to praise the dog over and over for her courage in saving Carroll. Gypsy woofed in pleasure, vibrating all over with pleasure and excitement. When Bronwyn stepped back into the house, Austin had returned and was leaning back against the counter, watching her with a lazy smile. "He has to be half bear," he said dryly.

"It's a she. And she's a Newfoundland, though I think she's half convinced sometimes that that's a breed of people." She pointed behind him. "The wine's for you." She hesitated. "And since you're rather stuck here because of Carroll, I do have enough for dinner, if you . . ."

One eyebrow rose, his eyes searing hers with an enigmatic expression. "Thank you. We were just going home to sandwiches tonight anyway."

"Good. Then if you don't like my makeshift meal, I won't have to worry about your going hungry."

For a moment he looked startled, and then he chuckled, a throaty sound of humor that made her smile again. Frankly appraising eyes settled on her smile, on the curve of her soft red lips, then up to the way that haunting sadness left her eyes when she smiled. "Tell me some more about that animal of yours. She's really a beauty."

While he leaned on the opposite end of the counter, Bronwyn went back to the kitchen, putting two plates on the counter with silverware, motioning for him to place them on the table. "Actually not. That is, I got sold on what an impressive beast she was, too, from the people I got her from. They raved on and on about her lifesaving skills. Which are true, as you know. But no one ever mentioned that she thinks the ocean is her own personal pool or that she feels obligated to wake me at five o'clock in the morning."

"You love her."

Bronwyn nodded, smiling. "I kind of feel the same way about five o'clocks and oceans."

He chuckled again, yet he was playing magnet games with his eyes again. She turned away. "I'm almost certain I've seen your face before," he said quietly. "The papers, I think. It's Bronwyn Laker Harmon, isn't it? The citrus industry?"

She reached for a sip of her wine. "Yes," she admitted absently. "Joe and I are divorced." One citrus dynasty, severed. She wondered vaguely why she had the feeling her money did not matter at all to him. It certainly bothered everyone else. Yet even if he was wearing a swimsuit frayed around the edges, she guessed he provided well for his daughter. She lifted the peas to the counter, then turned to stir the mushrooms in the frying pan. They were nearly done. "Maybe I should have warned you I don't exactly have a cookbook type of menu here."

He glanced at the dish of uncooked peas. "Is this normally the way you eat your vegetables? Not that I'm objecting—"

"I'm used to cooking just for myself. As in peanut butter sandwiches for breakfast."

"And dessert first," he nodded, with a slash of teasing smile. "Hermit's habits. For a lady far too beautiful to live as a hermit." She stiffened just a little at that compliment, her head down as she lifted the slices of ham to a plate. "Bronwyn?"

She half raised her head.

"What the hell am I going to do about her? Beat her when she wakes up or hug her to death? She's been told a thousand times not to go anywhere near that water alone."

She would have smiled again, warmed that he'd asked

24

her, almost amused by the grave bewilderment in his voice that had to be so out of character. Austin didn't strike her as the kind of man to suffer from indecision. Yet she didn't smile; the subject reminded her too much of another little girl who had fought for her life and lost in a hospital room. She brought the serving plates around, and motioned him with a swing of her dark head to bring the wineglasses. "You love her," she said simply, "with everything you have." She swallowed the lump in her throat, and then spoke again more carefully. "She's suffered enough, more than any scolding would do, don't you think? You'll be lucky if she isn't terrified of the water now." She hesitated. "But really, Austin, any advice from me is out of place. It's between you and your wife."

"Divorced two years ago," he said shortly as he sat down. The natural vibrance suddenly left his voice and a staccato crispness replaced it. "It was that or kill her. She was a beauty; you can see that in Carroll. All beauty on the surface and damned good in bed—with anyone. When I stopped loving the surface trappings, she tried that out—sleeping around. She did it one time in the house when the child was there. Left her crying in the crib. That was the time I knew I had to divorce her or kill her."

Bronwyn's fork remained suspended in midair as she stared at him. Unfortunately she believed him. The volatile potential was just . . . there, both the capacity for temper and the soul-deep sensuality. The only thing impossible to understand was why his wife could possibly have wanted to turn to anyone else. His cool blue eyes met hers. "I—what do you do for a living?" she asked helplessly.

"Caro and I have one of the little condominium complexes up the beach. The one we live in, actually. But what I really do is write." He speared a mushroom, then reached over to pour a second glass of wine for himself. "Sexy adventures. Not a hint of literary merit. When I was

25

a kid I was something of a vagabond. Anyway, they come easy and they make money. Nick Slolan's the name they use." She stared again. Nick Slolan. Bookstores were full of him—any bookstore. He glanced up at her. "Eat," he advised gruffly. "Then tell me what on earth you're doing holed up in this little cottage on the fringes of nowhere."

But her mind was still whirling. The way he'd rushed through his answers implied a desire to get the subject matter out of the way, as if he didn't mind her knowing but he didn't like to talk about himself.

Shadows lengthened on the terrace as they finished their dinner. At the door Gypsy stood, her head between her paws, half in and half out. A warm salty breeze wafted in. For no reason at all she felt comfortable with the silence between them. They'd covered the bases between strangers in a very short time; perhaps it was just time to absorb, let be. Perhaps, Bronwyn thought absently, he was just the sort of man who wasn't afraid of silences.

She picked up her empty plate, carrying it with her as she checked once more on the sleeping child. By the time she returned, Austin was shuffling plates to the counter from the dining table, one by one. The simple courtesy surprised her, more so when he actually came around to help. His palms loosely guided her hips out of the way of the open dishwasher, a gesture so intimate that it startled more than offended her. "I was just trying to get the plates to the dishwasher," he said lazily, but his eyes quickly skimmed over her again before he returned to k.p. "And I'm still trying to make sense of your being here all alone."

She wrapped up the ham, her eyes lowering momentarily as she set it in the refrigerator. That lazy appraisal didn't fool her. Energy radiated from Austin Steele, from his movements, from his eyes, from his deep, warming voice. From the instant she knew he wasn't married, she just couldn't seem to shake the funny feeling. "I'm just happy living here," she said finally, in answer to his question.

"Which makes no sense."

She hesitated. "I had a little girl. She . . . died." The word fell several thousand feet. Bronwyn lifted the last dish to the cupboard, her eyes averted. "Viral encephalitis. One day she was healthy, and seven days later . . . it was more than six months ago. I just wanted to be alone."

She heard him suck in his breath, and felt bad. She'd tried to make her voice light; there was no wish to make him uncomfortable. "How could your family have let you be alone?" he asked, his voice suddenly low and harsh.

"I didn't give them a choice." She found herself swiping at the counter that was already clean, over and over. "I wanted to be here. And it's . . . fine."

"Bronwyn?" But she couldn't look up yet. "Nothing like that is ever fine. You don't have to say that," he said gently. "And I'm sorry, very sorry about today. It must have opened it all up again."

"No. Really . . ." He took the cloth from her hand and tossed it into the sink. She felt first the hand on her shoulder, then fingers very gently chucking up her chin. The single tear was brushed from her cheek that she hadn't been able to help at the thought of Lorrie. His finger did it. Left a trail of warmth that somehow comforted, and she knew he wasn't going to pursue the subject she simply couldn't handle. He turned away, poured a glass of wine for himself, topped off her glass that she hadn't finished from dinner and carried them both into the living room. "So you dropped out, brown eyes, but six months is a long time. When are you going back to join the world?"

"Never," she said simply.

"Why?"

He took the center of the couch, his long arms stretched out on both sides. Bronwyn took the opposite chair, tucking her legs up under her. "There's no reason to," she said finally. "I came here to grieve for my daughter, but that healing has started to happen over time. It isn't Lorrie anymore. I just seem to see things differently from the way I used to. I just have . . . everything I want here."

He shook his head. "You know better than that."

She picked up her wineglass. "So says everyone. My parents, my ex-husband—"

"Ex?"

"Joe," she added. "And friends. I used to be a partner in an interior decorating business. The people from there too. At first there was a respectful silence, but lately the letters have been pouring in. Everyone's convinced that any second now I'm bound to regain my sanity and join the human race again." She hesitated, cupping her chin in her palm.

"If anything," Austin said slowly, "had happened to my daughter, I would have chosen to be alone, Bronwyn. Wanting no one else around. I wouldn't have wanted to smile for other people; I would have wanted to be free to just hurt. Like hell. To that extent I can understand your feelings."

Looking at him softly, she believed he did. She'd never phrased it that way in her mind, but that was exactly how she had felt at first. That she wanted simply the right and the freedom to hurt. And it just wasn't possible with other people around her.

"And when you bridge something alone," he continued gently, "you're stronger at the end of it." His eyes fastened on her with sudden fierce intensity. "Then comes the time when you have to prove it. By opening up again, by risking hurt again. By feeling again."

She looked down at her glass. "Perhaps." But it seemed to her that she had monopolized the conversation, and she took a breath. "Anyway, enough of my life story. If you've lived here any amount of time, you must have spent some hours around the island." Her eyes widened as he

28

launched himself out of the couch, coming toward her with an impatient look in those searing eyes. Didn't he like nice neutral topics for conversation? "I admit the alligators still have me intimidated, but they really stay in the lower part of the swamp. As long as you're on high ground . . ." He bent down, leaning two strong arms on the sides of her chair, and she gathered rather rapidly that it was a mistake to tell Austin Steele he was right about anything. "The first time I went into the lagoon . . ." she continued stubbornly.

His lips just brushed hers silent, his sudden close scent surrounding her like a fog. Again his mouth touched down, a gentle evocative testing of flavors, of textures. Her eyelids fluttered helplessly. There was no increase in pressure. Just that special softness, that sudden special silence, and the silken promise of his mouth like a secret shared between the two of them. His head rose, and she leaned her head back weakly in the chair, staring up at him.

"I've been a loner all my life, so don't think I don't understand, brown eyes," he said softly. "There are times when everyone needs to be alone, if only to develop an honest feeling of self-sufficiency, the knowledge that you can depend on yourself. And that's worth a measure of loneliness, though most people never see it. It's just not enough though, honey. Not for a lifetime."

His lips hovered again. Soft lips against the darkened grain of an evening beard. Heavy lashes shielded that depth of sky-blue eyes, and there was the way he brushed that tousled hair of his. The black chest hair against almost-brown skin, his Adam's apple, the cords in his neck. Her pulse was playing Latin rhythms, for a kiss that never happened.

"I think you already know that, Bronwyn. It shows in everything about you. And you should already have come to terms that there are still very definite needs that you can't fill for yourself."

They both heard Carroll's faint call for her father from the bedroom. Austin stood back up and then didn't move, his eyes holding hers in a hammerlock and then slowly shifting, taking in the tousled hair as it curved on her forehead, the silky shift draped to sensuous curves, her cocoa eyes and soft coral mouth. She knew he was willing to define those needs exactly. So quickly he'd stolen a certain power over her . . . and she resented it.

"I haven't missed a man," she said deliberately. "If you think because I'm living alone that I'm some sex-starved, frustrated little—"

"Bronwyn. I didn't say that at all and I didn't mean that." He was impatient again.

"You're implying that. And it isn't true. You don't know me at all, and I already have everything that I really need."

"Bull!" The growl was low-keyed, tinged with laughter.

CHAPTER THREE

The cottage was curiously quiet after Austin and Carroll left. Bronwyn puttered a little, making up the bed again, rinsing out Austin's wineglass. Her own was still half filled, and after a time she restlessly took it with her out to the terrace.

She was early for the sunset. Smoothing the ivory shift beneath her, she stretched out in the double hammock with one leg swinging lazily over the side, closing her eyes. Gypsy came close, nudging her head beneath Bronwyn's palm as if she sensed her mistress's unsettledness. The tangy salt air felt vibrant in her lungs, and after a time she opened her eyes to watch the colors in the sky. Mauve first, one of her favorites, and the most elusive to her brush and palette. The insects hushed; the birds stopped flying; the wind stilled. Greens softened as the night came on, taking on soft textures. When the sky was done with its sunset, Bronwyn rose again and walked down to the beach.

Quiet waves lapped in the incoming tide. A single gull soared down to fish, late for his supper, screaming when the fish successfully ducked for deeper waters. Sand crabs bubbled at the waterline and the sand sucked at her bare feet; the very faintest breeze was enough to stir the ivory shift, molding the silky fabric to her naked skin beneath.

She walked toward Merritt's peninsula, toward nothing and no one. She was safe hugging the shore, while inland, less than a quarter mile away, was Mosquito Lagoon, infested with everything from swarms of stinging insects to alligators. The birds were fantastic within the wildlife sanctuary; with proper clothing and insect repellent she was not a stranger to the island wilderness. She loved it.

Austin . . . he'd unsettled her; she couldn't deny it. But he was wrong. She hadn't missed people; it was as a loner that she felt she'd finally come into her own. The only communication she'd appreciated in these last months had been those from the lawyers. Succinct, crisp, emotionless. Sign here and return, Mrs. Harmon. You are divorced now, Mrs. Harmon. Enclosed is the monthly check from your grandmother's trust, Mrs. Harmon.

The Lakers were one of the most powerful families in the citrus industry in Florida, and had been so for several generations. There had never been any question that Bronwyn would attend a certain private school, that her friends would naturally evolve from that carefully cultivated group, that a marriage would happen to "one of her own kind." No one said any of the rules out loud; they were just understood from the time she was in the nursery.

Her talent in art was very nice, but interior decorating was a little more acceptable, if she had to choose a career. Her lack of interest in parties was understandable, but one had—obligations. The least sign of dissension and Bronwyn was pecked back affectionately into the brood. It was the kind of life she had led, following someone else's lead rather than upsetting the status quo, pretending to value things she hadn't, trying to feel things she didn't.

Fleetingly she thought of Joe. Unfaithful three months after their wedding, but she'd stayed. And still felt guilty over leaving him when Lorrie died. He was as grief-stricken as she was, and why should those infidelities have mattered to her now, when she had been silent for so long?

But she couldn't seem to pretend anything after Lorrie died. It all just seemed to crash. If one is good and obeys all the rules, there should be a reward. If she were the best wife by the rules she'd been taught, the best daughter, the best hostess . . . but the child died. It felt like having sold her soul for promises not kept.

There was just nothing there. Her job gave nothing back because she'd never really wanted it. No one was unkind. Her parents tried to offer her comfort, but how could they reach her when she'd never given them the least idea how she really felt about anything? And Joe—the marriage was long over by that time; it was only for Lorrie that it had ever held together, but it finally occurred to Bronwyn to put blame where it was due. She was the one who hadn't even tried to build a marriage with any real depth.

The woman she saw in the mirror in that grief-stricken period was shallow. Very tired of being pushed and pulled by other people's manipulations, very angry that she'd let it happen. Over six months she'd been forced to dredge up a sense of humor. To make a bed, fix a faucet, learn to cook, learn to be alone . . . twenty-eight was rather old for it. There were times she felt like twelve and times she felt like ninety. More than that, she no longer felt like shattered glass. Confidence had come from coping alone, from building a strength from within herself, from real pride. She was no longer a featherweight knocked this way and that by everyone's whim but her own.

Slowly Bronwyn stood up and started back. The soft sand was difficult to walk in, pulling at the muscles in her calves. The surf rolled over her ankles in ageless, haunting rhythms, the moonlight painting streaks of silver on the waves. She walked home, comfortable with the weariness invading her limbs, with the night's silence.

A half hour later she mounted the rickety wooden steps to her yard, absently brushing back her wind-whipped hair. A creak from a lawn chair alerted her, but still she was startled to see the gleam of dark eyes coming toward her in the night. Shadow took form—a sweat shirt and well-worn jeans, the deepset eyes . . . "You keep long hours, brown eyes. It's past midnight."

"It was a beautiful night." That comment came easy; from there she wasn't sure what to say. "Everything went all right with Carroll?"

"Fine. Mary's a retired pediatrics nurse, if I didn't already tell you that. Her only flaw is that she hates the water and it's Carroll's passion, but as far as my leaving her tonight, Mary's got a cot set up next to her and she's sleeping the sleep of the innocent. Unlike her father."

It was impossible not to take him up on that. "Unlike her father?" she repeated gravely. "Is your problem that you couldn't sleep like the innocent, or simply insomnia?"

"I owe you a decent thank-you. Stop making it difficult. I've been waiting for more than an hour."

"You don't owe me any thank-yous. You owe Gypsy a steak."

"I expect the T-bones are already buried in your front yard."

Bronwyn chuckled, yet she didn't move any closer, nor did she move her eyes from his. He was a great many things she was afraid of. Austin Steele, a man who could easily overpower, when she was never going to be overpowered by anyone again. He was too strong and too perceptive, yet she could feel a strange kindling in her skin as he approached, an electricity that made all her defensive instincts want to shift nicely by the wayside. She tried. Her voice was cool. "You didn't come here to deliver any thank-yous."

"No," he agreed, closing the distance between them with a deliberateness that she had expected. She knew he would come back, and if she'd guessed anything about the character of the man, he wasn't the kind to let her pack her bags and move out before he came after what he wanted. Still, when his palms slid up her bare arms she felt a shiver of shock. Honesty seemed a highbrow commodity

34

next to the texture of his hands ~~arms.~~ "I came back for my kiss, ~~one we were both thinking about~~

But still he waited. As he stood ~~hands glided up to her shoulders, trailing~~ ~~rial until~~ he found the warmth of skin ~~fingers traced her collarbone, then the thro~~ ~~her throat. Her flesh warmed and then quiver~~ the calloused skin of his palms.

She flicked back her hair, staring up at him. Moonlight hinted at the shadow on his chin; he had a cleft, strangely off-center. The night was the kind fantasies are made of— the sand silver, the ocean tipped silver, the moon silver. Silver, like the spun fabric of dreams. Austin was not that way. Austin was dark, like the night and his hair and his eyes. This man was not of dreams, not content with roles; he would never have tolerated the rules she tried to live by. "Austin, I . . ."

His mouth brushed her lips, silencing her. Like a sudden storm he gathered her close, his mouth searing on hers. One of his hands splayed in her thick luxuriant hair while the other roamed down to her hips. Shock echoed through her system as the tense hunger in his whole body communicated to her. Shock . . . and sweet pleasure.

Her fingers curled at his shoulders, then hesitantly reached behind his nape into the dark thickness of his hair. She'd wanted to do that from almost the first moment she'd met him, to explore the texture of that hair and the feel of his scalp, to know exactly what it would feel like to mold soft breasts to that iron chest. To just for once let go. To just for one minute to simply feel, to simply take what she wanted for herself . . .

And her touch was rewarded by the low growl she heard from the back of his throat, by the unbreakable mold he made of their lips together, by the sudden feverish pressure of his hands. It was cool suddenly, night cool on palms reached those thighs beneath her ... then moved to cup her bottom, cradling her ...erately to the hardness in his jeans, his kiss drinking in the weak murmured gasp in her throat. More slowly his hands shifted up to her spine, to the cool silk flesh of her back, and all that time his mouth never once left hers, his crazy moans exciting, distracting her. She felt possessed, taken over. As though her flesh were cherished and her secrets cradled between them in the night . . .

He finally lifted his mouth from hers. He clenched her shoulders, forcing a few inches of distance between them. She could still see the fire in his eyes, an effort at control in the tension in his body, a control she was struggling with in her own. "*That* was the 'simple kiss' you came back for?" she whispered, teasing him.

"It might have been simple. That was *not* the response of a lady content to live as a hermit the rest of her life," he retorted.

Her head bowed away from him, strands of hair flicking across her cheek in the breeze. "Is that why you came? To prove something?"

She heard his intake of breath and felt an incredibly tender brush of palm on her cheek. "No." Said so simply, she could not help but believe him. It was his turn to chide her. "I think you already knew better than that."

She lifted her chin, sudden confusion in her dark eyes. She thought she did. She thought she could trust her own judgment where she never had before. "I'm just not ready —for a relationship," she said quietly.

He shook his head at her, faintly smiling. "That won't go, Bronwyn. You want time to stand still and wait for you?"

"No." Her lips curled. "But I have the feeling you travel at the speed of sound. I don't know you, Austin. I don't really even know why you're here—"

"To be part of your life." That short distance between

36

them was closed again, a rough kiss planted on her mouth to remind her of the feelings they'd already created as a pair, whether either of them had really planned or expected it. "I want you," he whispered. "You're special, brown eyes. I knew it from the first minute I saw you. You want to tell me you didn't feel something just as powerful as I did? You want to just let it go?"

How was she supposed to think when he looked at her like that? She twisted free, running a shaky hand through her hair again. "Damn it, I don't know. Want, Austin? People can want you for a thousand things in a lifetime until the well's so drained, it's dry. I've been there, and I've turned into a very selfish woman these days. I want something back before I take any risks. You walk into my life by accident, and now you're starting something. If you want to walk right back out again, that's fine, but no one is just taking from me again, do you understand?"

A faint smile curved his mouth. Liquid dark eyes rested on hers. He bent to kiss her again swiftly, one of his hands lingering in her hair. "There's nothing more erotic than a selfish lady in bed, going after what she wants with no holds barred. Are you trying to turn me off, Bronwyn? Because your arguments are doing just the opposite to me." He shook his head, drawing away. "For tonight I really only did have a kiss on my mind. Just seeing you again. I have a daughter at home that I don't want to be away from for long, not this night, even with Mary right there. But if you'd be willing to walk back with me, Bronwyn. . . ."

"I'm trying to tell you I don't know what I want. I don't even know how we're talking about . . .

This is so fast. I wasn't offering; I wasn't even talking about . . ." She drew back from the magnetic touch, the pull an effort. She had the crazy urge to slap him; he was smiling the devil's smile.

"I'll be back," he promised. "Sleep tonight, Bronwyn."

CHAPTER FOUR

With her foot on the chair Bronwyn threaded the laces through her boots, pulled tightly, and tied them. They reached midcalf; she fitted baggy khaki pants inside. From the waist up she as yet was wearing nothing, but when the boots were tied she fetched a plastic container from the refrigerator, opened it, and splashed the cold fragrant liquid liberally on her bare skin. The scent was faintly like apples, a little sweeter. Another use for camomile tea: mosquitoes hated it.

Shivering, she pulled on a long-sleeved T-shirt. The day was hot outside, but the long sleeves were another protection against insects. The shirt was wrinkled, leaf green, and marvelously soft. A single rubber band captured her hair in back, out of her way. By the time she was back in the hall, Gypsy was moaning determinedly, leaning all 140 pounds rather obviously against the back door.

"Now, I told you you couldn't come," Bronwyn chided. "You think the birds are going to sit still for me with you there?"

Sad, soulful eyes followed her as she opened the closet next to the door, drawing out a sketch pad and pencils and placing them in a shoulder tote bag. "I'm not going to be that long. One little hour," she told the dog. Reluctantly Gypsy heaved up and out of the way. Smiling, Bronwyn reached for the doorknob just as she heard a knock on the opposite side.

Her visitor had thick silver hair brushed away from a well-tanned aristocratically handsome face. Broad shoulders were encased in a pale blue suit that matched his eyes, and though his age was over fifty, he wore his years like a statement of success and experience. "I don't know what you're doing dressed like that, angel, but you still certainly look better than the last time I saw you." He reached out and held her close, the scent of English Leather one she could have located blind in a crowd.

"Dad!" She drew back just a little, and covered her surprise with a little nervous laugh. "Of all the people I expected to see. What are you doing here?"

"Six months is too long, young lady. I thought I'd come and see this little cottage you bought. Well? Aren't you going to ask me in?"

"Of course, of course . . ." She dropped her art supplies, feeling the pitter-pat of nerves she always felt around her father. Although affection had always come naturally between them, her father still had the gift of making her feel a little off-balance. Theodore Laker was the kind of man who liked that edge, cultivated it, even with those closest to him. Still, they hadn't crossed swords in months now, and his familiar face . . . She tried to forget that sensation of nerves. "Can I get you something? Tea? Coffee?"

"Bronwyn, it's past noon," her father reproved, stepping past her with his hands on his hips to survey her living room. His glance lingered on the sketch of sandpipers over the couch, settled on that small *B* in the corner. "Gin and tonic and a twist of lime. Good view out here," he said jovially.

"Go see the rest," she urged.

She had his drink ready by the couch when he came back from the bedrooms. He leaned back with deceptive laziness, one leg crossed over the other as he studied his daughter with hooded eyes. He had the most potent smile of any man she'd ever known, and he used it freely on any female of the species—married or single, kin or stranger. "There seems to be some sort of animal sitting in your shower," he commented dryly, downing half the glass in several gulps. "I assume it's tame."

Bronwyn chuckled. "At least she looks the part of a good watchdog. Did you notice?"

"I noticed." He finished the glass just that quickly, and set it down. "You're more beautiful than even your mother. Did you know that, angel?"

Something in the compliment made her smile hover. "Do you want another drink?" she asked quietly.

"A little stronger on the gin," her father asked. "Then we'll talk, sweetheart. Do you know how long it's been since just the two of us were together—no Joe, no your mother, no anyone?"

She knew. Those father-daughter moments were exclusively reserved for those singular occasions when the powers-that-be considered Bronwyn might need a little persuading. The drink she made was shallow and weak, though she added a spoonful more gin on top to fool her father as to its overall potency. She knew him.

"Why don't you slip into something pretty while you're at it, honey?" Her father called out to her. "Where were you going in that crazy outfit anyway?"

"To the swamp," she responded. "To sketch some birds. Dad, I've seriously taken up painting again—"

"That's nice." As interested as gray skies. Still, her father smiled his most charming smile as she served him the drink.

Bronwyn went into the bedroom. Swamp-wear was exchanged for white pants and a black silk shirt and lipstick was added. Clothes on a woman mattered to her father; she could not remember a time she had ever seen her mother without makeup. Changing her clothes was not the old token of obedience this time but an acknowledgment that he had driven the two hours to see her. And if

40

he'd come to make war, she felt strong enough to meet him halfway.

A few minutes later it started, once he'd finished his second drink and she'd sipped at her own sun tea. "Will you just let me speak my heart out without interrupting?" he pleaded boyishly.

She curled a leg beneath her, cupped her chin in one hand, and felt old ghosts shadow her chair. "Of course, Dad."

"Fine." The charming smile faded, the warm blue eyes iced over and the words were spoken with staccato harshness. "I don't know what the hell you're doing in this fool little cottage when you know damn well you could have had the beach house. I don't even think you do. Like it was all nothing that you've dropped out of a successful job and social career and marriage—and don't tell me Joe wanted the divorce. I know better. He may have let it happen, but then we were all afraid you were going to break if we looked at you sideways when Lorrie died. I loved that child, too, Bronwyn, but she damn well isn't coming back, and as for this isolation, the no-phone communication, drawing birds for heaven's sake, I've had enough of it! You could have Joe back in a minute if you'd just come to your senses." He waved his hands. "Skip that. The point is, I want you *home*. This has been going on long enough. For nearly seven months I've been damned patient—"

"Not seven, Dad, four," Bronwyn said calmly. "For three months you had a gentleman living a few houses down from me that I would have sworn retired from Laker's." She almost smiled sadly. "You never read a letter I sent you, did you?"

For a moment her father looked speechless, then lurched up like the businessman he was, towering, ruthless, a man who'd been manipulating people for several decades. His voice lowered just perceptibly. "Your mother and I want you to come home, to see a good doctor. Then

41

if you still 'need time,' I'll send you to Europe if you want. Paris, for clothes. Then the islands . . ."

"Dad, no, thank you," Bronwyn said softly.

He glared fiercely at her. "All right. The trip was your mother's idea anyway. I just want you home. I'm even willing to go so far as to get you an apartment close by, until you're on your feet again."

She hadn't felt this sort of emotional weariness in months. "I *am* on my feet. And I'm twenty-eight," she reminded him unhappily. "Dad, I have my own money, my own means of support. I love you and Mother more than you can ever know, and I know you don't understand, Dad, and, God, I'm sorry for that, but—"

"Don't you start swearing," Theodore Laker said sharply. He shook his head, changing tactics. "I hate to have to say this, Bronwyn, but you're going to cause your mother a heart attack."

Someone was rapping on the door. Gypsy woofed from the depths of the shower and came waddling lazily out as Bronwyn got up from the chair to answer it. To her disgust there was a blur of tears in her eyes. Give in . . . she'd always done it. And her father was only getting warmed up.

She opened the door, and her eyes were suddenly on a level with a riot of dark curly hair on a distinctly masculine chest. The cutoffs exhibited a full decade of wear and tear—tight, ragged, and low-slung. Dark glasses hid Austin's eyes, but his thick black hair had been wind-tossed, adding to the image of a thoroughly comfortable, totally disreputable . . . and one hundred percent masculine man. In contrast to all of that, he had a plastic pail and shovel in one hand, and in the other the small palm of one tear-stained child. "The plan for today was a solid fifteen hours at the typewriter. Somehow more important priorities developed." He gently squeezed his daughter's hand. "Much more important priorities." He looked up, saying in a low

42

voice, "We seem to have run into a little problem when we came within an inch of the water. If anyone would understand, Bronwyn, I thought you would. And Caro said if you came down to the beach with us—"

She nodded in total understanding, though seeing Austin, after last night, started a little erratic pulse in her throat. She hadn't begun to sort out her feelings for him yet, and it didn't help that her father had just started a guerrilla war. Not looking at either man, she simply crouched down, dredging a smooth finger across the child's wet cheek. "Hello again, Caro," she said quietly. "I'm happy you came to see me."

"Hello," the little one echoed back. "Will you come with us?"

She glanced back up. The men above her were bristling like two male toms entering the same territory: eyes held over the distance, smiles were glued in place, alertness was written in the stiffness of the shoulders. "Mr. Laker, I'm Austin Steele." A hand was extended.

The hands met over Bronwyn's head, but her father was shaking his head. "I swear the name and face are familiar, but I'm embarrassed to say I really don't remember. Have I met you before, Mr. Steele?"

"I don't believe so, no."

"I didn't even realize my daughter here knew anyone in the area," Theodore Laker said jovially.

Bronwyn sighed irritably, then trailed after Carroll. Predictably the girl had gone in search of the dog, a mutual choice as it happened. Gypsy was displaying a long spread of stomach and the child was stroking her obligingly. Bronwyn knelt down again. "Listen, darling. My dad came to see me today, and I haven't seen him in a very long time. I would love to come down to the beach with you, but I just can't. Would it be all right if I came and got you first thing tomorrow morning?"

"Bronwyn. It isn't like you to disappoint a child." Startled, Bronwyn looked up to her father's suddenly easy smile. She stood up warily. "I've always got a bathing suit in the car trunk, you know that. Take the child down to the water, by all means. Austin and I will make a pitcher of drinks and come down and join you."

"Now, look, Dad." She knew exactly what her father was thinking. An "unchecked out" man had dared to enter his daughter's sphere. The game didn't amuse her. At seventeen perhaps she needed the protection; at twenty-eight the tears were already dried. She read through her father's charm, and she was closer than she had been in years to completely losing her temper. "I think we'd just better get our little talk over with. For both our sakes."

Her father managed to look blank. "We can talk anytime, Bronwyn," he said smoothly. "We can finish our conversation when I take you home for that matter—"

"Dad, I am home."

"Bronwyn?" The little redhead tugged at her pants. "Come with me!"

"Of course you're coming home with me today. I just told you about your mother," her father said pleasantly. "And did I tell you that Joe's been asking about you? Your mother and I had him to dinner—"

She all but lost it; a scream of frustration echoed inside her head. "Joe who?" she snapped tautly, knowing the answer just as she knew her mother was in perfect health.

"Your husband," Theodore grated.

"I'm not married, Dad. For that matter, even if the papers were signed only last month, we haven't lived as man and wife for over two years. So whatever you think you're implying—"

"There's nothing to get upset about, angel. Listen, I'll be right back." The moment her father turned away, intent on going back out to retrieve his swimsuit from the car, she felt a silent slap, like hot metal, on her backside.

Shocked, she felt Austin's strong arm around her shoulder, steering her past the doorway crowded with child and dog, past the hall and into her bedroom. Two dried swimsuits were lying on the bed, waiting to be put away. He motioned to the white maillot.

His hand released her shoulder, suddenly gentle, and then he headed for the door. "So your father throws you, Bronwyn," he said bluntly. "That's not news. He throws half the men who think they run this state. He plays down and dirty, and he wins. That's not your league. Keep in mind that you don't necessarily want to play in that league, and it might be easier."

Bronwyn closed the glass sliding doors with a snap, sealing her father and Austin distinctly on the other side. With a cumbersome straw hat on her head and her arms laden with towels, she made her way down the steps to the beach, Gypsy cavorting ahead of her and Carroll just behind. "I want to go down to the beach, but I don't want to go in the water," the child reminded Bronwyn.

"Who said anything about swimming?" Bronwyn asked lightly. "I had in mind building sand castles." The feeling of tautness inside faded. The child deserved more than that.

"Or could we dig great big holes?"

"Huge ones!" She laid down the towels, glancing up to the steadily beating sun. It was the hottest part of the afternoon, a fluff of clouds only occasionally blocking out the brightness. Far down the beach she could see a smattering of cars in front of the condominiums, but around her cottage there was no one. "We'll have to work really hard," Bronwyn said casually.

So they worked very hard, although digging holes was postponed in favor of burying Gypsy, certainly no easier a task. They both laughed when the dog finally groaned with all the patience that was required of her, lurched up, and shook off her blanket of sand as she galloped to the water. The hole project was started then, with Bronwyn deliberately setting the pace, watching from the corner of her eye as the first beads of moisture showed on the child's forehead. The sun baked down, hotter and hotter. "Water's beginning to look pretty good," she said idly.

Carroll glanced once at the ocean, then shook her head violently.

"Okay, darling. Let's just keep on."

The men had come down by then, carting Bronwyn's lawn chairs from her terrace. They set them a distance from the water, and whatever negative vibrations she'd expected from the two men alone together just weren't happening. She could hear her father's full-blooded laughter and Austin's huskier evocative chuckles. *Why didn't I realize before that I hated men?* she thought vaguely. Her father had come for the express purpose of upsetting her apple cart. The "apple cart" was intact, though she very definitely still felt upset. Now he wasn't so much as glancing her way. And Austin, his rough words about her father had left her feeling both hot and cold. The warmth, from his perception, from his intrinsic understanding of how and why her father upset her, his stepping in and taking over. The chill came from his high-handed way of doing it, and he wasn't looking in her direction either.

She was looking in his, and was disgusted with herself for the way her eyes were continually drawn to him. Austin was the uncut stone next to her father's polish, the honed blade next to her father's sheathed steel. Seeing the two men together unwillingly invoked a whole trail of thoughts better left buried. She could not help but be aware that it was the very earthiness of Austin's looks that appealed so to her, that she had never been drawn to the kind of distinguished looks her father had, not in the core of her. Raw sexuality touched the same in her. It was something she'd known for a long time—known, acknowledged, and shelved. Caveman attractions were not something one built one's life on.

Still, there was an unwilling glimmer of respect that Theodore Laker obviously didn't throw Austin—he had certainly always thrown Joe. Both clever and ambitious, Joe could hardly wait to bring a good idea to her father, but he would back down like a wounded puppy if Theodore criticized him. Austin wouldn't give a damn. She knew it without having to hear or watch Austin, but from watching her father—the way he sat, the way he looked, the body language—he communicated clearly the distance. Respect was being exchanged, if not liking.

Bronwyn stood up, her forehead dripping from the heat, and glanced again at Carroll. "Sweetheart, I am absolutely boiling. Aren't you?"

The child nodded. Bronwyn walked to the water's edge, barely getting her feet wet, and made a big commotion of splashing all over. "That felt terrific!" she enthused as she came back to the child. "Shall we go just a little closer to the water so we can build a sand castle?"

The child considered. "Could I cover you up instead?"

"Of course. But I have to sit here where it's a little cooler, okay, love?" Not waiting for an answer, Bronwyn stretched out with her legs in the surf, leaning with her arms back. Not needing an order to be protective, Gypsy sat in about five inches of water between ocean and child, letting the waves splash all around her. Tentatively Carroll approached the water with her bucket and pail, glancing frequently at the crashing waves.

After a time she was so absorbed in burying Bronwyn in heaps of sand that she forgot about the water, giggling as Bronwyn groaned, and laughing as Gypsy barked in the distance. Without even being aware, Carroll was sitting in the shallow area, totally soaked, as happy and carefree as she had been the day before the accident.

Theodore Laker paced the distance, gazing impassively

47

at his totally disheveled and sandy daughter. "I've got to be getting home, Bronwyn."

"Oh, no!" Bronwyn wrenched up, looking first at the sandy mud caked to her legs, then down at Carroll sadly. "How on earth am I going to get all this off? We can't go up to the house like this!"

"I know." Absently Carroll looked out at the water. "But . . ."

"Angel," Theodore said impatiently. "You can play these games some other time."

"Actually I don't think so," she said pleasantly. Priorities was one of many arenas they totally disagreed on. As much as she wanted to finish the talk with her father, Carroll was four, and her experience of the day before rated more than halfway measures. "You just start up to the house, Dad, I'll be right there," she said shortly. His look was impatient, but he turned away. To the child she said, "I already know you don't want to get in the water, sweets. It's no problem. We'll just try to get clean this way." She brushed, ineffectually, at the crusty sand, and Carroll mimicked her actions on her own little sand-covered body.

"It doesn't work," the child said lamely.

"Well, if we just went in and splashed . . ." But a lazy effort at splashing from the shallow waters obligingly produced only more mud. "I just don't know . . ."

Several seconds of silence passed. "If you carried me in," the child finally offered tentatively.

"Oh, I think," Bronwyn said with a radiant smile, "that we can manage that without any problem at all!"

A few minutes later they ran the width of the beach to Bronwyn's wooden steps, both soaked to the skin and laughing from their dip in the ocean. Her father was standing with Austin on the cement terrace, and had already had time to change back into his business suit. Carroll ran for her father to be tossed exuberantly in the

48

air by Austin, but his eyes were for Bronwyn, warm and emotive. "Thank you," he said quietly. And to his daughter, "And this morning you told me you didn't want to go swimming anymore. Who did I just see floating in those waves?"

"I wasn't swimming," the child corrected him. "We were getting cleaned. There's a difference, Daddy."

"I see. . . ."

Smiling, Bronwyn turned to her father, her eyes losing a little of their natural warmth. "If you would like to stay for dinner . . ." She felt compelled to make the offer.

His smile was wry as he bent to kiss her wet cheek gingerly. She was shedding water from the swim, hair dripping in her eyes with a thorough lack of regard for her appearance, something she wouldn't have been able to do at seventeen, or even a few months ago. Being comfortable with whom she was instead of what she looked like she'd only learned since she'd lived alone, though she didn't expect her father to relate to that.

She walked with her father to his car, waiting while he bundled his bathing suit into the trunk and fished his car keys from his pocket. "I don't want things to be difficult between us, Dad," she offered tentatively. "If you want or need me at home, you know I'll come. But here is where I'm staying, where I'm living—at least for now."

He got into the car and put the key in the ignition, closing the door with that same fixed smile. "I'll be in touch," he said absently. "Soon, Bronwyn."

For Theodore Laker to so readily back off confused her. "I hope you're not still angry. I know you don't understand, Dad, but—"

"But I do understand, darling. And between the two of us, everything's going to be just fine." He touched her hand affectionately, and she released it from the open car window. In less than a minute he was gone.

49

CHAPTER FIVE

Theodore Laker never shifted into neutral. Still feeling rather bewildered at his sudden change of attitude, Bronwyn started back up the steps to her cottage. She ran a brush through her hair before coming back on the terrace.

Carroll had the outside shower turned on the dog; the child was squealing delightedly as Gypsy woofed appreciatively at being sprayed. Austin was watching the pair with hands on her hips until Bronwyn appeared in the doorway. As if by a sixth sense, he turned, eyes shuttered in the harsh afternoon sun, to see her sleek fall of dark hair contrasted to the damp and clinging white maillot, the soft expression in her eyes as they rested on the child.

She glanced up when he approached her, the smile for the child including him. "She's so beautiful, Au—"

His arms threaded beneath her cloak of hair as he bent down, his mouth gently rubbing on hers. From the chill dampness of her swimsuit she could feel the heat of his body, an intense heat from being in the sun for so long, a vibrant heat that felt like it would burn her cool skin. He drew back a little, but not so much that his face didn't shadow hers from the sun. "Thank you," he said quietly, "for getting my daughter back in the water."

"I . . ." He had the strangest eyes. Light blue with huge pupils and a fringe of heavy lashes, a soft arresting color next to his leathery skin. "She's still afraid," Bronwyn said weakly. "I think she still should be afraid; a certain fear of the water is important too, Austin. In time she'll go back in on her own though. You could see it." He was smiling at her babbling. He reached up, and with a finger traced the line of her jaw, ending with his warm hands loosely on her shoulders. A shiver of sheer sexual awareness ran through her bloodstream, of the potent attraction this man had for her. "I—what did you say to my father?" she asked. Why didn't she just move?

His lips dipped once more, and she realized disgustedly that her face was raised in anticipation. It was a smile he pressed on her mouth, swift, strong, and fleeting. "We talked about a lot of things. We were sitting on the beach for over an hour," he said.

She did move back then. She had a curious feeling of disorientation; the child was right there, her familiar front yard with its hammock and chairs and shower and century plants. And her father had just left, had upset her a great deal before they had gone down to the beach. It all seemed to disappear when Austin touched her, and Austin seemed all but a stranger. She'd lived alone a long time now, was not even sure she knew what to expect anymore being around people. She did know that feeling like melted butter was basically insane. "You must have said something to him," she said more stiffly. "When he left he was in a completely different mood."

Austin glanced again at his child. Carroll had turned off the shower and was in the process of climbing into the hammock, her little bottom wiggling in the air as she struggled to get in. Gypsy nudged her and she catapulted into the canvas, giggling. Bronwyn smiled again, too, the world returning to normal again.

"When we got past that I had no designs on your future, needed no paying off, and could skeet-shoot as well as he could, then we were down to one cold-blooded bastard speaking to another," Austin said absently. "We've both played the same game of ball, Bronwyn, just in different stadiums. I told him his daughter needed an affair to shock her back to real life."

"Pardon?" She was still smiling, certain she had misheard him.

"He was furious." Lazily Austin rubbed the back of his neck, watching her reaction. "But I think by the time we were done talking he recognized that the kind of emotional upheaval he was in a position to hand out to you wasn't going to budge you from hibernation."

She stared at him, shocked and then angry, and feeling a strange warmth inside at the blatantly sensual look in his eyes. They were both diverted when the child tumbled over the side of the hammock with a startled cry. Bronwyn reached her first, but Carroll was still laughing as she was pulled to her feet. "Gypsy's thirsty. Terribly."

"Gypsy's thirsty, is it?" Bronwyn said dryly.

"For a glass of milk," the child enlarged, nodding vigorously.

"I think we'll make do with a glass of water, Caro, while Bronwyn gets dressed. We're taking her to dinner."

"Goodie!" The child leapt into the air. "McDonald's, Daddy?"

"Actually I had in mind something a little more digestable."

"You like McDonald's, don't you, Bronwyn?" The child folded her palm inside Bronwyn's as they headed back in the house.

"I certainly do," Bronwyn agreed, adding swiftly, "but I'm afraid I just can't go to dinner with you. Your father takes a great deal for granted, I think."

Ignoring Austin, she and the child went into the kitchen, where Bronwyn first unearthed a cookie from the cupboard and then poured a small glass of milk. Austin came around, leaning against the doorway, to her mind, blocking it.

"So I scared you off?" he asked mockingly, his hands

52

stuffed lazily into his cutoff pockets, eyes searing hers. "You didn't like it put into words, brown eyes?"

"You had no right to say anything like that to my father," she said stiffly. *Or to look at me that way.*

"The dinner, specifically, was to thank you for what you've done for Carroll in the last two days."

Not to encourage the affair he'd just mentioned to her father? She leaned back against the counter a distance away from him, watching the child thirstily gulp down the glass of milk. "You *have* thanked me," she said cheerfully.

"I want some more," Carroll requested.

"Say please," her father directed.

"Please."

Bronwyn opened the refrigerator again to bring out more milk.

"Is she going to dinner with us, Daddy?" The girl whispered.

"Bronwyn has to take it slow and easy," her father whispered back. "Just like getting you back into the water today. But you went back in, didn't you, punkin? Bronwyn's still sitting on dry sand."

The child shook her head bewilderedly. "Bronwyn went in the water with me, Daddy. Didn't you see?"

"Yes, I did," her father answered, looking at Bronwyn.

"Do you know," she said furiously, stung that he had accused her of cowardice, "I've been managing amazingly well all by myself. I'm even capable of deciding what I need and don't need in my life. It just might be that I simply don't want—"

"It's there every time I come close to you, Bronwyn. Don't tell me what you don't want. Just because you don't have the courage to say it out loud."

"You're wrong. I go after exactly what I want in life these days. What I don't do is get bulldozed into doing anything," she retorted tightly. She turned back to the child. "Done with your milk?" she asked mildly.

53

The child nodded, handing her the empty glass, and then ran to the backyard to fetch her pail and shovel, dragging a towel behind her. Bronwyn would have followed her if Austin hadn't hooked her waist and half turned her to face him before she could . . . dissemble. Lazy and slow he laced his fingers behind her nape, the weight of his wrists heavy on her shoulders. She seemed to be breathing in that sunwarmed flesh. "Austin . . ."

"Feel it? I don't even have to touch you," he whispered slowly. Her eyes were troubled, a resentful dark brown when they met his. He was touching her. His eyes made a sweeping seductive caress that she could feel beneath her clothes, beneath her skin, and the feel of his fingers languidly tangling in her hair made her ache with longing.

His hands dropped; one arched eyebrow said he'd made his point. "Dinner, Bronwyn," he repeated. "That's called a chance to talk; there's no seduction going on when a four-year-old is dropping french fries."

But she turned away deliberately to the child. Carroll was cavorting around with her beach gear trailing, and Gypsy was just behind her, her tongue lolling out. No, there was no seduction in that scene either. Except for what she felt whenever she came in contact with him. She bent to kiss the child good-bye. He just went too damned fast, and the last two days had been too crazy.

"We're at Briarwood, a half mile down the beach. One seventeen. When you decide you're ready, brown eyes . . ."

"I'm very happy alone, thank you," she told him curtly.

But she wasn't. During the next few days she couldn't seem to settle down. She did all the normal things, almost daily invading the swamps with her sketch pad. A prize-winning artist in school, the first time she'd picked up a brush again was when she moved here, beginning with an oil of Lorrie. Now her spare room was filled with canvases.

Whimsical colorful bird figures, the lagoon and beach, characters she glimpsed in passing. Her skill had improved as rapidly as her own personal life, yet that was not really the point, she'd told herself for months. The work was only intended for her own eyes, her own need for self-expression.

Yet that didn't seem to wash anymore. There seemed, strangely, little purpose doing anything solely for herself. And the herbs she'd been studying—the finding, storing, studying their natural healing properties, like her favorite, camomile—as a hobby had absorbed time. She loved the growing and the learning, but somehow it was not the same.

She had no phone, no TV, no radio. She hadn't wanted them. *The Wall Street Journal* kept her informed; her stereo played her favorite blend—some days classical, some days jazz. Emotive, the music. Emotive, the sensual fabrics she continued to wear on bare skin. Emotive, the long silent nights and the ceaseless rhythm of lonely surf. She couldn't seem to sleep, a restlessness causing long midnight walks with the dog at her side.

She couldn't get the blasted man out of her mind was the thing. She felt stirred up, like someone thrown out of a warm bed on a cold morning. She didn't even like him. He moved too fast, had a possessive air she didn't appreciate—and God knew, she had had enough of domineering men in her lifetime. He was the takeover kind; she wasn't in the market. She'd never handled relationships with men in her life very well; it just wasn't worth all the emotional upheaval. . . .

But he'd been a bastard to accuse her of cowardice. She hated that label. Alone, she'd found the courage to cope with the agonizing grief after Lorrie died. Alone, she'd forced change on herself, painful growth. And she felt whole; she knew she had changed. But all that was suddenly very easy to say from her vacuum; Austin was life, real life. And in those long silent nights "too soon" only rang out like an excuse; she knew she wanted to see him again. Sheer physical desire was part of that, but not all. It was the man himself, and that for the first time in her life she glimpsed the possibility of an honest relationship. Honest and equal, with a man she wanted to understand, with a man she felt already understood her too well. . . .

Austin was deliberately banished from her thoughts a few nights later. With all the lights turned off and the stereo on low, Bronwyn was curled on the couch in peaceful silence, just listening. It was just after ten. Gypsy was lying by the open glass doors, and wind was whipping up the salt air outside.

Suddenly Gypsy whined. Her head jerked up from a sound sleep as she stared intently out the open door. "What's wrong, sweetheart?" Bronwyn asked idly.

The dog stood, the silky hair on the back of her neck rising, a low menacing growl coming from the back of her throat. Frowning, Bronwyn put her bare feet on the carpet. When Gypsy snarled again, her heart skipped a beat in involuntary fear. Moving silently in the darkness, she tiptoed behind the curtains to peer out.

The hammock was rocking; from the distance she could see the silver froth of the waves. It was a moonless night, clouds bunching together above, the wind drowning out other sounds. She could see no one. The dog lurched over to her, rubbing restlessly against her leg, and then went back to stare at the open door with a single piercing bark.

Truly frightened now, Bronwyn belted her arms under her chest, glancing at the back door. It wasn't locked. She never locked it. It seemed a very long mile of pitch dark room to get to that lock, and for the first time she regretted that she had no phone; there was no way to call the police.

Gypsy started to growl now in earnest, letting out

56

rough, menacing woofs in warning, pacing back and forth in front of the door. "You *stay*," Bronwyn ordered in a commanding whisper. The dog too rarely showed any nervousness for Bronwyn not to believe her; there was something wrong.

There were shadows everywhere, with the wind tossing up leaves and branches. Still, Bronwyn could discern no human shadow, and she finally forced herself out from the curtain's shadows to hurriedly push the doors closed and lock them, her heart pounding. The dog's barking increased in frenzy, so loud and furious that Bronwyn could barely think, much less hear anything over the din. "Shhh!" she commanded, but Gypsy was beyond obeying.

Hurrying to the back door, for an instant Bronwyn thought she glimpsed a man's shadow at the kitchen window; Gypsy reacted, nearly bolting up on the sink to reach him. Bronwyn leaned against the back door, perspiration beading on her forehead, her hands suddenly shaking. From the drive she vaguely thought she heard the sound of a car revving its engine, but with all Gypsy's noise she was not sure. "Quiet!" she repeated to the dog.

She crouched down, and most unwillingly the dog came to her in the darkness, shivering all over with tension. "Easy, easy," she urged Gypsy, but there were no more sounds of a car. The house was dark, but she was still afraid of turning on a light for fear of showing herself. Dressed in a man's long red T-shirt that she'd planned to sleep in . . . well, it wasn't the way she would have chosen to meet a stranger, much less a prowler. Gradually Gypsy quieted after pacing one more time around the cottage, finally settling with a decided thump on the carpet by the glass doors, as if the entire episode had wearied her.

Abruptly Bronwyn switched on a light and switched off the stereo, starting to draw all the curtains and shades, trying to calm herself. "It could have been a kid walking the beach," she scolded Gypsy. "Just anyone. Someone who ran out of gas, or a camper from the island." Besides which, she reminded herself, she had the 140-pound dog. There was really no conceivable reason to be afraid even if it had been a prowler; no one would have braved that dark house with Gypsy barking unless he had been insane.

Rational thought was all very well. She repeated all that to herself as she insisted Gypsy accompany her to the bedroom while she closed those drapes, snatched up panties, a light pair of jeans, bra, and a long-sleeved navy silk shirt that should have been paired with a business suit. Her fingers were trembling. Gypsy was impatient at being pinned in the bathroom with her while she ran a brush through her hair, and shocked black eyes just stared at her when she pulled out a leash. Bronwyn put back the leash, and went from room to room turning on all the lights.

There was no one, of course. The doors were locked; the dog was with her. She had nothing to be afraid of. It was probably someone who had run out of gas or was just walking, and had given up when he'd seen no lights and heard the dog. Yet Gypsy never took on like that. . . .

Still, she walked back to the glass doors in the living room and forced herself to open the curtains again. The black darkness had no appeal. "All right, no leash," she told the dog. "But stick close, do you hear me?"

The dog whimpered, anticipating her walk. Bronwyn opened the door and felt her heart leap in her throat at the total darkness, the silence so eerily muted with the sounds of the wind and the surf, with shadows. The two raced helter-skelter for the beach, and then walked. And walked . . .

Fear gradually worked out of Bronwyn's system as she convinced herself there was simply no reason for it. Yet, as she retraced her steps from the island back toward her cottage, she found herself unwilling to return home, and kept walking, Gypsy loping at her side. For the first time since she'd moved here, she found herself resentful of the isolation, aware of her own loneliness. She just didn't want to be alone, not on this night.

Her pace didn't stop for nearly a half mile past her cottage, where Briarwood Condos lay sheltered in leafy privacy. It was not a large complex, but it was expensive and tasteful, with expansive landscaping surrounding the two mammoth pools. Bronwyn saw no one as she made her way up the private walk. Gypsy couldn't seem to figure out why her mistress was in such a sudden hurry, yet Bronwyn didn't stop until she reached 117, and from a single window saw light. At least Austin wasn't asleep.

She hesitated at the door with her hand posed to knock, and then, instead, rapidly combed her fingers through her hair to restore some order to it, standing limply, looking at the dog. "So should we go home?" she asked Gypsy weakly. "You don't have to tell me this isn't exactly the hour to go visiting anyone."

Go home. To her cottage in the middle of nowhere, to her life that seemed just as suspended in the middle of nowhere.

She knocked resolutely at the door, willing her expression to calm.

Austin opened it with a half-filled legal pad in his hands, his leathered complexion wearing a distracted frown. He had the sort of beard that required twice daily shaving, and there was a shadow of darkness around his chin, his hair in rumpled disorder. His jaw half dropped at the sight of her and the dog, his eyes narrowed in immediate and assessing alertness. Jeans and an old red sweat shirt cloaked his masculine figure . . . in a way. The jeans were old and molded softly to his muscular thighs, and the soft fabric of the sweat shirt pulled up on his arms accented the distinct curl of black hair on his arms.

She smiled hesitantly in greeting, not having any idea how vulnerable her huge brown eyes appeared, how wildly erotic she looked with her mane of dark hair in disorder. The silky blouse molded to her breasts, made worse when a trembling hand moved to smooth, all too conscious that she must look a mess. "Hi," she said weakly. "Just your local hermit come to call. I know it's late. I was just walking by and saw your light, Austin."

"It's about time," he said brusquely. "Come on in, brown eyes."

CHAPTER SIX

Austin closed the door behind them as Bronwyn stepped in. Gypsy lost no time in settling promptly in the hall, underfoot. From there Bronwyn could just glimpse a portion of his living room. Rust and cream furnishings blended with the warmth of books from ceiling to floor; a long low coffee table was spread with papers and legal pads, a cup of coffee still steaming in the middle of them. Soft lighting, warmth, and a man's flavor, a man's textures—she took it in as a single impression, but it was the coffee table where her eyes rested. "You were working, Austin. I didn't mean to . . ."

There was no one listening. Austin had disappeared into a side room she assumed was the kitchen. She walked in just a little farther, and then stood, rather nervous. The desire was to explore the bookshelves, to study the feel of the room Austin lived in, to touch and examine it. She didn't. Instead, the sheer quiet and comfort of the room reached out to her—or tried to.

She jumped when she felt Austin's hand on her shoulder, and pivoted to find a drink in his hand. "Cognac," he said shortly. There was that slash of a smile she remembered, but she could feel he was still assessing her. "Find a comfortable spot if you can." He bent down to collect up the papers on the coffee table while she curled up obediently in the closest chair and raised the glass to her lips.

"Is Carroll asleep?" she asked idly.

"No. She's out on the beach playing tag at eleven o'clock at night. Just relax, Bronwyn. Something happened, didn't it?"

She nodded, thoroughly irritated that he was so perceptive, and stared down into the amber liquid she suddenly didn't seem to have near as much need of. Whatever lingering fear had still been harboring in her system disappeared. It was enough, being here, by him. And she knew that was why she'd really come, not because of any apprehension because of the supposed prowler. "One can get enough of isolation on occasion," she admitted quietly.

"I'm glad you're here." He hesitated, as if wanting to pursue that, as if measuring whether to pursue exactly what had happened to bring her here at this time of night. Instead, he stood up and held out a hand. "Come on, I'll show you around. Mary's got the condo next to this one. We've got a door fitted between the two, bordering her bedroom on Caro's. That way if I'm gone at night I just open it and I know Mary will hear her." His eyes met hers, as if he could see the conclusions she was drawing in her mind. "Although, truthfully, I'm rarely gone at night. Or haven't been in some time."

"I didn't ask," she insisted softly.

"Didn't you?" With his hand at the small of her back, she walked ahead of him, carrying the cognac. A light was already on in his den, on a desk holding both a typewriter and stacks of typewritten sheets that said he was in the middle of one of his books. Behind was a credenza with an expensive computer and printer; behind that were bookshelves, filled floor to ceiling. Rust carpeting and dark paneling accented a feeling of quiet and privacy.

"You're prepared to do all of your work from here, aren't you?" she asked.

He nodded. "Everything but the research."

"And where do you get your ideas from? They're all adventure stories, aren't they?"

"When I was a reckless idiot of a kid, all I wanted to do was see the world, from Alaska to the South Seas. So I did."

She waited a moment, expecting him to expand on that more than interesting little statement, but all he did was walk to the door. She shook her head at him, smiling. He was so very brusque when talking about himself. "I did interrupt your work tonight, didn't I?"

"I work a lot at night because of Caro, and, yes, you've completely destroyed my concentration," he agreed mildly. "But, then, I'm more than willing to switch focus and concentrate just as intensely on something else. The look of you, for example. What exactly brought you out of hibernation tonight, for example. What—"

"Austin!"

He stopped speaking but didn't seem inclined to let her back through the doorway until he'd brushed her hair back with his fingers, restoring his own personal brand of order to it that the ocean wind had whipped up. "Did I tell you I was glad you came?" he whispered.

She shook her head, laughing up at him. "You're deliberately trying to make me nervous."

He disagreed. "I'm doing a very good job of making you smile. When you came in the door you looked ready to fly back out before you'd even said hello." He led her back out to the hall, automatically lowering his voice. Again she thought fleetingly that he was just a little too sensitive to her feelings for her own comfort, yet she couldn't seem to help liking the lazy, easy warmth he sent out like vibrations. Had she really been scared out of her mind by prowlers earlier? Because at the moment, next to him, she found it difficult to imagine being afraid of anything.

He motioned to Carroll's room, and she peeked in to see a pink and white decor overlaid with toys, and a small, silent mound under the covers. She caught a glimpse of his darkened bedroom, then two bathrooms, a dining room, and a kitchen, then a small utility room. The colors were tasteful and the place had a lived-in warmth that Bronwyn liked; the stamp of Austin's personality was in the unique layout. "I love it," she said honestly as they walked back into the living room. "But I can't believe every one of the condos in the complex is this special, Austin."

"Each one is different—completely different in layout, though overall of a similar size. I've got good people, mainly because I went out of my way to find people I wouldn't mind as neighbors. And as thrilling a subject as that is, Bronwyn . . ." He leaned over the chair she had settled in so comfortably, looking very much as if he were prepared to pin her there for a very long time. "What happened?"

"Nothing." She lowered her eyes and took a single sip from the cognac.

"Something did."

She nodded softly, her dark eyes mirrored in his. His demanded honesty, and Bronwyn, for the first time since she could remember, reflected both the desire and the need to be honest. "Yes," she admitted quietly. "It was really nothing, Austin, but afterward I started to think of exactly how isolated I've really been. I just . . . wanted to see you. Nothing more," she added carefully.

Absently he reached down to push back a strand of hair from her cheek. His fingers lingered, his palm cupping her chin just for a moment, and unconsciously she leaned to it. "I've been hard-pressed to give you time, brown eyes. No matter how much I've wanted to see you again, I was hoping you'd leave the fortress on your own." He stretched back up, and looked at her so intently that she felt like shivering, but, instead, smiled a little nervously.

"Originally I left the 'fortress' over a ridiculous set of nerves," she admitted ruefully. "Would you believe I talked myself into believing there was a prowler simply because Gypsy decided to do a little baying at the moon tonight? But that really isn't why I came, Austin. I kept thinking as I was walking . . ." His expression had changed so abruptly that she found her words trailing off, her smile hovering midstream.

"You thought there was a prowler and yet you took off alone on a deserted beach in the middle of the night?"

She blinked, rather disoriented at his suddenly furious tone. "It wasn't like that. I mean, there are campers all the time on the island, for one thing. There wasn't anything to worry about. Even if there really had been someone there, there was no one by the time I left. I thought I heard a car drive away—"

It appeared to be another wrong thing to say. "Damn it to hell. Why didn't you phone—" He drew an exasperated breath. "You don't *have* a phone. Well, you're not going back there, Bronwyn. You can stay here tonight. I'll go back to your place."

"Actually I'm perfectly capable of checking out my own place, but if I ever need a bossy bodyguard—" She lurched up from the chair.

"Bronwyn, we are not going to argue," he growled.

"We certainly aren't. I told you there was nothing—"

"And I'm telling you you're not going back there alone."

"Look," she began furiously.

He started toward her with such determination that she faltered. The kiss he pressed on her forehead was soft as a cotton puff, as tender as a feather's brush. She stared up at him, bemused. "Are you going to wait for me while I open Mary's door and find my shoes?" he asked mildly.

Very reluctantly she smiled, and then they both chuckled. She was going nowhere without him. He knew it, and so did she. Though every instinct warred at being brow-

65

beaten, and though she knew it was foolish, she really didn't want to face the empty cottage alone.

When they were out in the open wind on the beach, he slung an arm around her waist and eased his palm into her back pocket. They walked in unison as Gypsy raced ahead, the salt wind stinging at both of their faces, whipping up their hair. She liked the feel of the intimate hand in her back pocket and curled closer, with her face in the cradle of his shoulder and her own arm around his waist, feeling the rhythm of his hips as they walked. They could have been lovers on the deserted beach, and the ocean's roar urged an erotic pulse inside Bronwyn. She looked up only once, and found immediately his lips ready for her raised face. The kiss was hard, potent, and fleeting; he never broke stride. The taste lingered, warm brandy mixed with his own special flavor. It was there, just as it had been before, the most powerful sexual yearning she had ever known touched off in her life.

They both paused at the top of the wooden steps to her yard. Austin's jaw hardened; his hand suddenly tightened on her wrist. She glanced up.

Someone seemed to have left every light in the place on, though she couldn't remember doing it. Certainly she'd never in her life run out the glass doors to the patio and left them wide open. Austin just looked at her.

"Someone has to support the electric company," she tried lightly.

"Tell me again how Gypsy was just baying at the moon, brown eyes. You forget, I've seen you in a crisis. You don't shake up easily. Gypsy." The dog, startled, turned her shaggy head at the definite command. "Stay by Bronwyn."

"Look. I admit I overreacted a little—"

"Do you think you could make me a sandwich?"

She stared up at him blankly. The last thing on her mind was cooking.

"A BLT if you have it. Gypsy!"

Bronwyn was pushed rather inelegantly through the door to the kitchen and the dog nudged to a warden's position in the doorway by Austin's hand. She glanced at his retreating figure helplessly. Bacon—at this hour? It took ages, and the dog was becoming such a turncoat, taking orders from anyone these days, even riffraff. She didn't really mind his checking out the inside of the house, closet by closet, but rather unconsciously her imagination went into overtime when he stalked outside. What if someone *was* still out there?

There was a spatter of rain on the glass doors when Austin finally returned, locking the door behind him and pulling the drapes. His hair looked blue-black, with just a glistening of moisture on it, and as he bent down to begin switching off half the lights that beaconed the entire house, she glanced up from her fork and frying pan. There was a tight expression on his face that made her want to look away, wondering vaguely if a prowler wouldn't have been easier to handle than Austin in a real temper.

Blotting the crisp bacon between paper towels, she added the strips of lettuce and reached for the tomato slices.

"You haven't got one decent lock on any door or window. The one bolt you have a baby could break. The place hasn't got a decent shutter for the storm season—you do know we get hurricanes at this time of year? There are shingles loose on the west side, and as far as your break-wall, lady, it should have been repaired a decade ago."

So. There really was absolutely no one out there. She pushed his plate to the other side of the counter and turned on tiptoe for the mugs in her cupboard. Cognac was all very well, but peppermint tea might actually soothe his nerves.

"Did you hear me?" he demanded.

Bronwyn tossed Gypsy her single strip of bacon and

added honey to the two teacups. "I love storms, and the house has obviously withstood a few years of weather without collapsing before I bought it," she said mildly. "And as far as bolts, this is hardly a high-crime area, Austin. Any self-respecting burglar would have gone for the condos, not this little cottage. Now, I already admitted to overreacting earlier—"

"Are you getting new locks tomorrow, or shall I?"

She set the frying pan in the sink and squirted in soap. "If you'll stop sounding so belligerent, I'll get them."

"And a telephone."

"I don't . . . yes."

She'd shied from contact with the outside world, but, no, it didn't matter anymore. She'd really known that from the day her father had visited. Perhaps she never would overcome his ability to upset her, but that wasn't the same thing as fearing she would just give in again. She didn't need to run anymore. Or hide. From anyone.

"Suddenly so obedient, Bronwyn? What's going to happen?"

She lifted the pan from the water, wiped it, and took his empty plate. "If you have a spare eight by ten of yourself —preferably glossy—I wouldn't mind setting up a dart board. Now, I'll admit I'm grateful you checked out the house, Austin, but we don't have to keep dwelling on it. I feel enough like a fool as it is."

"All I'm asking is whether or not you want someone to spend the night with you, Bronwyn," he said mildly.

He was talking about fear, she knew that. She considered what it would feel like to be alone that particular night, and felt no fear of any kind. She considered the undercurrents between them, the look in his eyes. She considered the rain now pelting down, the half-mile walk back to his home, and that Carroll was already taken care of. She considered the cognac and soothing peppermint tea in her system, and when she was through working all of that out in her mind, the only thing that mattered was that she knew she had stopped running.

"Yes," she murmured.

"Yes," he repeated dryly. "On the couch, I take it, brown eyes? Or is there even a remote possibility . . ."

He was trying to tease. She switched off the kitchen lights and just looked at him the distance across the counter, and suddenly he stopped teasing, the look in his eyes turning dramatically different.

He was beside her in seconds, roughly reaching for her in the darkness. "You're crazy," he murmured gruffly. Her lips parted; she received his kiss with a hunger that surged through her, like something wild just let loose. She clutched his hair, molding her supple body to his. He was ballast, the real world, human . . . he was shelter, understanding, strength. Those things mattered. Not tomorrow. Not dictionary definitions of love. And for just this once she claimed the right to reach out for herself, for what she needed.

His hands smoothed up and down her sides, fingers splayed, exploring the feel of the silk blouse against her skin. Their tongues twisted together, dark secrets exchanged, the kiss ending only when they were both breathless. For a moment then they stood in the dark, looking at each other, waiting for something more manageable than erupting volcanoes and that heartbursting fierceness. More gently his lips pressed on hers and then slowly trailed a sensual path into her hair; his hands came up to thread through that silky weight in the darkness, got lost in it.

Just as slowly she ran her hands up and down his arms, loving the supple give of muscle and hardness. Gently she traced the hollow in his throat and his collarbone, then explored the roughly erotic bristles of beard on his chin. At his waist she slipped her hands under the smooth sweat

69

shirt, lingering slowly as her fingers moved up over a rough chest. There was no self-consciousness; it was part of the insanity. There had always been a reticence with Joe. Not now. It didn't belong, not with Austin. Absorbed, she felt the erratic throb of his heartbeat, then smoothed her hands back down from warm vibrant flesh to the rougher texture of his jeans. His hips were narrow, taut, more taut as her hands kneaded them restlessly, and she heard his gravelly intake of breath.

"Bronwyn." Austin stilled those hands, and gently tilted her chin. Smoky brown eyes stared up at him, wildly impatient and sensually lazy, a blend that could exist only in one arena. "Stop."

She shook her head.

"As in now. As in five minutes ago," he whispered roughly. "Because I can guarantee I won't, Bronwyn. You were upset tonight. Believe me, if you still feel the same tomorrow—"

"Shut up, Austin," she murmured. "This isn't for you; it's for me."

"Oh? Are you using me, brown eyes?"

"Yes." She reached up on tiptoe to kiss that hint of a smile. "Yes." His smile disappeared. And Bronwyn was suddenly trembling.

The bedroom was dark when Austin shut the door. Outside, the rain was pelting against the glass doors of the balcony, black-greens glistening strange night shadows within. The silence was such a sudden thing, a memory of a hundred lonely nights blending with a crazy feeling that she had just touched flame, but that was not the same thing as dipping her hands into it. It was a stranger who silently undid the silk buttons of her blouse. In a moment it slipped to the carpet around her feet. He took off his belt, then weaved hers out of its loops, his lips grazing her neck as he half bent over her. His slow, gentle movements built an unbearable tension; she couldn't stop trembling.

70

Austin was nothing like Joe. The only man she had ever known was Joe, and she had never felt this fierce, wild feeling, a sudden fear that she knew nothing.

Slowly his hands threaded in her hair, tilting her face up to his. It was not a stranger's eyes that looked down at her. She had known him—forever. The look kindled flame and her throat arched back. His lips tasted hers lightly, teasing her fear, coaxing her to relax. As if he knew . . .

"I'm not afraid," she whispered.

"You won't be," he agreed. He drew her close, locking that strange sensation of trembling within warm strong arms, holding her to his chest. The beating of his heart was like the steady rhythm of a clock, a pulse that first soothed and then seemed to roar in her ears. There was nothing else. Just the gentleness of touch and a whisper's blend of a man's special scent surrounding her. Austin's scent.

Her eyes, closed, opened on his. Her arms curled around his waist and she found his mouth in the darkness, waiting for her. She felt drawn into a spiraling vortex—the pressure of his mouth, the taste of him, the feel of her breasts crushed against the dark hair of his chest, the mold of thighs together. In another world there was a storm, a dog moaning its isolation, an ocean that never ceased its movement.

His breathing was uneven when he finally lifted his head, and his thumb softly trailed the shape of her trembling lips. She touched his face in return, her eyes never leaving his as his hands strayed to the clasp of her bra in back, as she felt the thin straps slipped from her shoulders. So slowly his hands trailed up from her ribs to the weight of her breasts, pearled in the darkness, firm, aching. He cradled each in his hands, bent to kiss each, at first softly. "Aren't you beautiful . . ." he whispered roughly. The nipples shied under praise, tightened and tensed; he was

71

not content with that. His teeth nipped, then soothed with his tongue until the sensitive flesh softened and swelled.

"Austin . . ."

He reached for the snap and zipper of her jeans, his palms gliding down the skin of her hips to encourage them off. She was lifted to the cool sheets while he took off the rest of his clothes; she watched, with dark luminous eyes, the naked beauty of the man, the slope of thigh and the tightness of buttocks, the long expanse of golden chest illuminated in darkness. Their eyes met, and in a moment he was beside her, covering her, flesh on flesh, and a rush of sheer wanton heat was freed inside of her, wild, haunting, intense.

"Austin . . ."

He was reality. Knowing him. His flesh, his eyes and hands, the taste of him. His pride, his hunger, the way he took control, the moments he lost it. She had been married a long time. She felt as though she had never made love before. Her skin felt warm, then hot, then coated with silk. She felt the full stretch of his body on top of hers, then hers on top of his; she kept hearing the sound of her own breathing, shallow, erratic. His flesh was as velvet as her own, the softest film of moisture cleaving them together.

It was a tender invasion, his possession. She felt her whole body open for him, felt the hollow ache of desire filled like her spirit felt filled, with passion, with joy. For a moment he didn't move, cradled inside of her, his arms tucked under hers and his hands in her hair. "I love the look of you," he whispered. "Right now. Just like this."

She reached for him, drawing his head down, drawing his lips down to hers. She whispered back, of joy and desire, of her need for him as his body took on the fierce rhythm of loving. He knew the same song; he sang it back to her in the way he moved, the incredible way he made her feel. She felt wind-tossed, carried high, her body filled,

72

her spirit soaring. Shudders suddenly encompassed her body, an explosion of pleasure.

He held her, trembling, wondrous, close to his breast until they both slept.

CHAPTER SEVEN

Sunlight streamed through the coral drapes, shimmering a pastel haze on the entire bedroom. Bronwyn opened her eyes lazily, first aware of Austin's arm tucked protectively around her, and then aware, reluctantly, of the dog's head resting on the edge of the blanket, eyes wide and pleading in her direction. She glanced back to Austin's sleeping face, loving the unusual softness of his features in rest, and then carefully slid out from the warm cocoon of blankets with a silencing finger on her lips for Gypsy. Naked, she tiptoed to the curtains, peered out long enough to insure no one was in sight on the beach, and opened the door to let the dog out for her morning run.

The rain had washed all the greens clean, calmed the ocean. The steady lap of surf on the shore had a light-hearted rhythm, and the gulls were just swooping down for their breakfast.

"I seem to have lost one very warm-blooded body," Austin complained from the bed in a husky whisper. "Get back here."

For a moment a smile of embarrassment wavered, and then with a radiant exuberance she pounced back on the bed, and on hands and knees crouched over him, bending to kiss his rough-whiskered jaw. "I hate to have to admit this, Mr. Steele," she whispered, "but I am marvelously happy!" She nipped playfully at the tip of his ear, taking a larger bite of his shoulder. "You have no idea how

74

absolutely wonderful I feel. None. I'd go into a great deal more detail, but I'm just afraid it would all go to your head."

He snatched at both her hands, twisting to gain some control over her playful teeth. A stern scowl riveted his brow, spoiled entirely by the mischievous warmth in his blue eyes. The scolding was spoiled by the kiss that accompanied it. "I've never heard such scandalous talk from a lady raised in a private Catholic girl's school. You're supposed to be an inhibited little package of rigid moral codes. Didn't the nuns ever teach you not to wear patent-leather shoes so the boys couldn't see up your skirts?"

"They did," she agreed solemnly, delighting in the ticklish sensation of his lips in the curl of her neck. "They taught us all kinds of guilt to keep us good. I just don't know what happened. . . ."

"You are, Bronwyn," he whispered. "Very, very good."

She blushed then, something she hadn't done in years, knowing he wasn't exactly talking about the same kind of good she was. At the color in her cheeks he chuckled wickedly, and in retaliation she burrowed the covers back and drew a slim fingernail down his side. He burst into immediate laughter, and before she could continue she found herself pinned with her arms above her head, his response to the most minor of offensives swift, totally unfair, and completely distracting.

An hour later she was still sleepily entwined in his arms, wondering how it was possible to feel so absolutely natural with him. She had no feel for tomorrow, but she already knew she could not have any regrets for yesterday. As a lover he almost frightened her with the soul he put into his lovemaking, taking everything, giving everything, obliterating inhibitions she hadn't even known she had. And as a friend, after they'd made love for the third time, that feeling had come into play, too, secrets shared she'd never shared, crazy little things she'd never thought to tell anyone. He had so much perception, knowing when to be sensitive and soft with her, knowing when to bulldoze through with a question she was too shy to answer. She'd never known any man to accept her just for who she was, not within the roles of hostess or businesswoman or even wife, but just the human being.

"I have to get up," he murmured. "I've got a mountain of revisions to do today that has to get done. And Carroll's fine with Mary, but they're bound to be wondering."

"You'd better get up," she agreed, snuggling closer to him.

She heard a sound in his throat like a hoarse chuckle. "You're *not* helping."

"I am too. I'm keeping you warm until you get up."

With another chuckle he lifted himself up and then crouched over her, smoothing back the wanton curtain of her dark hair. Her lips were reddened, almost bruised, from their long night of loving, and her complexion had the intimate burn from contact with his rough skin. Sensuous eyes looked back at him, loving the intimate feeling of his chest hair against her breasts, of the look in his lazy blue eyes. "You make a very poor case for a hermit, brown eyes. How you managed to live alone this long . . ."

She had lived her entire life alone, she felt like responding. There had never been anything like last night for her, never a man like Austin for her. She opened her mouth to say something, and heard a sharp rattle of the door from the other room, followed by Gypsy's frenzied barking. Startled, she jerked up, as did Austin.

"No one comes here," she said. "Even my father—not at this time in the morning. I . . ."

The fear of the prowler from the night before was suddenly with her. Austin bent down to swiftly kiss her lips. "Relax, Bronwyn. Would you rather I answered it for you?"

"Yes . . . no." She changed her mind, hearing again the

76

wild barking. "If Gypsy . . ." Obviously she would have to handle her own dog. In seconds she pulled on a pale rose caftan, and ran her fingers through her hair as she hurried out. Austin, behind her, was pulling on the jeans and the sweat shirt he'd worn the night before.

She pulled open the door with her fingers still in her hair, wearing both a curious and an apprehensive expression on her face. "Gypsy," she scolded, even as she was looking up to see who it was.

Before she could say anything, the man was inside, pushing closed the door with Gypsy all but slammed on the outside. "For God's sakes, Bron, what the hell kind of animal is that? I tried to knock on your door last night and changed my mind after hearing that growl. Of course you need some kind of protection, but I can't imagine she attacks anyone who just approaches your door in the broad light of day—"

"I—she doesn't," Bronwyn said weakly. Nervously she touched her fingers to her temples. "So it was you last night. It never occurred to me. I—why are you here?"

Joe Harmon had the build of a golfer, long, strong legs and a deep, even tan. His blond and distinguished good looks were accented by the tan suit he wore with a pale blue Oxford-cloth shirt. Always well-groomed, today was no exception, but apart from the shock of seeing her ex-husband again, Bronwyn was taken aback by his appearance itself. Deep hollows smudged dark beneath his eyes; he had lost at least twenty pounds, and his easy, charming smile seemed nowhere. "I have to talk to you," he said quietly, almost desperately. "Please, Bronwyn. I stayed in a motel last night. I have to—"

"Are you ill?" she questioned, worried. For whatever had happened—or never happened—between them, she had never wished him ill. He was Lorrie's father, for one thing, and for another, when the chips were all down for her when she'd first come here, she had accepted most of

77

the blame for their failed marriage herself. She felt no bitterness; only a lingering sadness at times.

Yet, it wasn't sadness she felt at all when she saw Joe's eyes. She half turned to see Austin emerging from her bedroom. Joe suddenly looked directly at her as if she were a stranger, taking in very conclusively her bruised lips and disheveled hair, the rose caftan that concealed everything but the fact that there was nothing beneath it. His lips glued together in a rigid line.

Austin, in contrast, wore a lazy half smile and a look of concern. "Harmon?" His outstretched hand was ignored. He dropped it, moving past Joe to the kitchen with a single brush of his fingers on Bronwyn's shoulder. "You look as if you could use a cup of coffee. You nearly scared the wits out of Bronwyn last night. She thought she had a prowler."

"I see. So you just stayed to watch out for her," Joe said evenly, with just a tinge of bitterness.

The sally was ignored. Austin dropped down to his haunches, closing and opening cupboards until he found the instant coffee. Joe stayed just where he was in the doorway, staring down at her, and Gypsy set up a frantic howl to be let back in.

Bronwyn wondered vaguely if there was a pit she could conveniently crawl into, and decided instead that no one had to face this kind of horror without at least claiming the right to brush her teeth and have some decent clothes on. She motioned Joe into the living room, and made tracks to her bedroom.

Less than fifteen minutes later Bronwyn returned to the living room. Her hair was brushed and pulled back with an apricot scarf; a blouson top matched that, gauzy and fresh, and the dark brown slacks fit comfortably without being too revealing.

Austin was leaning forward on the couch with one hand on a steaming mug of coffee and the other hand clenched on Gypsy's collar. The dog leaned her heavy frame against Austin's leg, but she was facing Joe and the hair on the back of her neck was bristling, standing up. Joe was in a straight chair opposite, eyeing the dog warily, not touching the coffee cup on the table next to him. No one seemed to have anything to say, but both looked up when Bronwyn entered the room.

She had the immediate desire to go back in the bedroom and stay there. The warm loving in Austin's eyes was gone, replaced by something neutral, cool, and definitely distant. She didn't know how to explain that she hadn't seen Joe in six months, that their marriage was over an aeon before that, that she never expected his visit or wanted it, or that she suddenly felt like crying.

And Joe . . . she moved her fingers to her temples as she looked at Joe. He looked so dreadful, and though she fiercely resented his unexpected intrusion, she also felt guilty because of that. If too much of their eight years had been shallow, they were still eight years, and knowing how she must have looked to him at the door . . . The mornings after they'd been to bed she'd barely had a hair out of place, which was undoubtedly why he'd turned to other women. They had never shared that kind of electricity, but she would never have chosen to slap his face with it.

"Bronwyn." Austin set his mug down. "Take your dog."

"Oh . . . I . . ." She scrambled, delighted to do something, although she was not exactly certain why she was snatching at Gypsy's collar until the dog, freed from anyone's hold for approximately two seconds, produced a menacing growl in Joe's direction. "Gypsy! I—she's always so friendly, I . . ." The dog had never shown a moment of temperament before.

"Out," Austin commanded the dog.

Whimpering, the dog slipped through the glass doors

79

Bronwyn had opened, and she closed them firmly afterward. "I'm sorry, Joe. She must still be thinking of you from last night, that you were a . . . I've never seen her behave like that."

"Yes," Joe said curtly.

Bronwyn hesitated.

Taking the coffee cup with him to the counter, Austin said pleasantly, "I'll be going. Have a good day, Harmon. Bronwyn."

She trailed after him with stricken eyes. If there was some black comedy in all of this, she missed it. "Austin," she said helplessly.

He stopped just outside the back door. "Feed him some breakfast, Bronwyn. It looks to me like he needs it, and badly." The kiss on her forehead was swift and impersonal. "And put some color back in your face. He's your business, not mine."

"But I don't want you to—"

"It's your affair, Bronwyn," Austin repeated, and then with a distant slash of a smile, "but I have to say I'd keep Gypsy well away from him." He turned to go.

His attitude made no sense to her. Nerves were shredding her stomach into tiny little acid balls; he certainly showed none. There was no sign of jealousy—or even of being uncomfortable. The night was over. It wasn't that she'd expected lifelong commitments. But shouldn't he have shown something toward the man she'd shared years with, if he cared at all? How easily he had just up and . . . left.

Distressed and distracted, she went back into the house. Joe had risen by that time, was staring out at the ocean.

"I—would you like some breakfast?" she asked uncomfortably.

Her nerves settled as she made the small meal, and the two of them ate with the sun streaming down on the table. She waited patiently to find out why he had come, but instead Joe seemed insistent on talking business, the firm he'd joined to get out from under the family harness, how the citrus was faring this year, weather and groves. It was a world she had grown up with and knew well. She put Austin out of her mind because, simply, she had to. And certainly Joe acted as if he had just walked in and started talking, as if there had been no fifteen-minute interval with another man there.

While she washed the dishes he came to stand in the doorway to watch her, a tense expression on his face that distracted her. "What would you be doing if I hadn't come here today?" he asked when she finished wiping her hands.

She shrugged. "Walking the island. Sketching, probably."

"Let's do that then, Bronwyn."

Joe took off his jacket and tie while Bronwyn went to find some canvas shoes. His starched shirt and Italian shoes were still inappropriate wear for the areas they would walk, but she didn't want to embarrass him by saying so. Obviously he wanted to talk to her away from the cottage, yet she was startled he even offered to do something she wanted. Even when she was successful as a decorator, he never asked her the first question of how she was doing or the problems she had had on the job. Her hobby, he'd considered it, as she obviously had no financial reason to work.

She offered him some mosquito repellent, which he shrugged off. A few minutes later they were walking the sandy road inland toward the island. Rough scrub marked both sides of the barely drivable road, and all signs of human habitation disappeared within fifteen minutes. An occasional marker showed a path that might be of interest in the national wildlife refuge. To the right was Mosquito Lagoon, where one could rent a canoe to cross in and out of the swamp and lake. If one were prepared to cope with or ignore the rougher elements, such as snakes, mosquitoes, and alligators, there were some of the most fantastic flowers and birds. Still, it was not, she knew, Joe's cup of tea.

To the left was hilly scrub, cactus and waving greenery; paths in that direction ended at some time at the beach. Straight ahead some fifteen miles was Cape Kennedy. The sun beat down Florida-style on both of them, the humidity rising as the heat of the morning backed into the sandy road. Joe had a film of perspiration on his forehead that ashened through his brown tan, and again Bronwyn felt concern that he had been ill. He opened his shirt, swatting at mosquitoes, but he simply moved ahead of her when she tried to slow their pace to accommodate him.

When he finally did start talking, it came out in a rush.

"I keep thinking about Lorrie, Bron. I keep thinking about how you looked the day she died. I don't think I've slept in weeks. I keep working; I play golf; I do all the things I've always done, but I keep thinking about her."

"Oh, Joe," Bronwyn said compassionately. Her heart ached with the same bitter sweetness she always felt when she thought of her daughter . . . Joe's daughter too. "I know," she said gently.

"No," he said roughly. "You don't know how I feel, Bronwyn. I gave you the divorce because I knew you were going to get it anyway. It wasn't what I wanted, but I felt I had no choice. But it's been a long time without you, and I've had nothing but time to think. I'd like to say I didn't resent that man this morning, and I know damn well it's none of my business anymore. God knows I did it to you often enough, didn't I?"

The naked emotion in his face was a man in torment; Bronwyn was almost frightened by it. "Yes," she agreed quietly. "You did it to me. It doesn't matter anymore."

"It does matter," he said fiercely. "I was a bastard to you. I never tried . . . we played at a storybook marriage, didn't we, Bronwyn?"

"Yes," she agreed uncomfortably, looking away.

"But that wasn't all of it. Lorrie wasn't storybook love. We both loved that child; that was real. And when we lost her . . ."

Helplessly Bronwyn stared at the sleek-winged egret that landed in a clump of brush not far from them. Her eyes blurred in remembered pain, tears helplessly welling in her eyes.

"It all changed for me, Bronwyn. I'm not the same man. I'd like to . . . see you again. I want to try to build something real this time. I think we could. I think we almost did, in Lorrie."

Startled, she looked back at him. His hands were shoved into his pockets, and again the naked anguish radiated from his taut features. None of the self-confidence or ego-tistical charm and smooth talk of the husband she knew were there. Compassion touched her, and for a moment she waited, almost wishing for his sake to feel even a glimmer of the love she once thought she'd felt for him. It wasn't there. But the look of his expensive trousers and now-wilting shirt, the effort he'd made to walk her turf when the mosquitoes and heat were digging at him . . . "Joe, I just don't think, . . ." she started very gently.

"Don't say no. Think of Lorrie, and how she looked, and how beautiful she was. Don't say no, Bronwyn. All I'm asking is to see you again. To spend some time together. Just to see. You have to give me a chance," he pleaded harshly.

She stopped trying to walk. Turning away from him, she closed her eyes for one long desperate moment. He was changed; she could see it. And he'd touched at her weakest point—Lorrie, his child too. A bond that could never be broken. It was the only bond she felt inside, but because of it her heart reached out to him in compassion, in empathy. When he was laying his soul bare, she did not know how to tell him that there was simply no love there.

83

She hated having the power to hurt him; she didn't want to hurt him. She just wanted . . .

Austin's face appeared beneath her closed eyes. She wished him here. She wished him here and she wished she were alone with him, in their own private world. Her eyes blinked open. Of course he was not. And from the way he'd left, she wasn't really certain he even wanted to be with her. The night had been offered freely; they both knew that.

"Go out to dinner with me tonight," Joe coaxed. "Just one night, Bronwyn. No strings. Just a good dinner and some wine. I promise I won't bring up anything else. You don't even have to think about it."

No, she thought. *Please don't ask me. I can't help you, Joe, don't ask me. All my life I've let myself be pushed by other people's wants and needs.* But she looked again at his haggard appearance, at the pallor beneath his tan. "One dinner, Joe," she said slowly. "No more than that."

CHAPTER EIGHT

The restaurant was in Daytona, the kind of place where she and Joe had always spent a fair amount of time together, a country-club atmosphere with white linen tablecloths, the tinkle of crystal, and subtle background music coming from somewhere out of sight.

Joe ordered for her—lobster, her favorite, with a white wine she knew would be excellent. Wine was a hobby of Joe's, a suitable hobby for the elite, she thought fleetingly, and then dismissed the uncharitable thought. Joe was doing his best to be his most charming, and he was certainly the most handsome man in the room in an impeccable white suit and a tan shirt. The wind had rumpled his hair just a little from the walk inside. She knew if he were aware of that it would annoy him, but as it was he looked oddly boyish and certainly all-American. Even the haggard lines and weight loss were less apparent under the flattering dimmed lights.

"You've never looked better, you know, Bron," he complimented her, eyes subtly appreciating her emerald dinner dress. "For one thing, you never used to spend all that much time in the sun, between working and Lorrie. The rest has done you good, and I've always known you'd look terrific with a dark tan."

"I wasn't working that much when Lorrie was little," she reminded him absently. "I just could never see wasting whole days at the country club just to work on a tan."

"No. You all but had to be dragged there, didn't you, love? And you fought the idea of a nanny, which at the time I could never understand; I thought you'd want your free time. But you not only liked being a mother; you were a damned good one."

"Joe," she started uncomfortably, setting down her wineglass.

"Unlike my own mother," he said smoothly the moment the thread of impatience entered her voice. "I remember I showed up for one of my mother's teas one day after playing outside all morning. I brought her a mud pie. I thought it was beautiful, a most cherished gift. She accepted it just like the lady she was, but I don't think I saw her again until I was twelve. I was promptly removed by my faithful nanny, Mrs. Bartholomew . . ." He rolled the name on his tongue, finally raising an unconscious smile from Bronwyn. "She wore glasses with rhinestones and toddled a bit of brandy in her tea—four or five times a day. She was good fun by bedtime but carried a real whip hand first thing in the morning. If I didn't toe the line, I was locked upstairs—God forbid with her."

"Joe! She couldn't have been that bad," Bronwyn cried, looking at him curiously. Joe had never spoken that way of his childhood; after living with him for so many years she had never had a hint that his young years were anything less than happy. "Why didn't you tell your parents about the drinking?"

"Why? She was almost livable when she had a buzz on."

She shook her head, half laughing, knowing he was trying deliberately to entertain her. Pushing her dinner plate aside, she dipped her fingers into the hot lemon water served in sterling, and then wiped her hands on the linen napkin.

"Marietta misses you," he mentioned over coffee. "She did the Swanson house—you remember it, Bron? That big old white elephant? Over two million just for the furnishings alone. A good commission, but she said you were really the only one who could have done justice to the blend of periods she wanted."

"Hasn't she found another partner yet?" Bronwyn asked. The tall svelte blonde had been interesting to work with, with a marvelous head for business and a way of convincing most people she knew exactly what they wanted. It was Bronwyn who carried out the actual color and period designs—a job of research, footwork, and a clever eye, and not the creative focus she'd hoped would be in the work. But, then, Lorrie had been able to go with her a great portion of the time, and the two women had made a surprisingly good team by bringing together two completely different sets of talents.

"I think she's holding out for you to come back," Joe said carefully, studying her over his coffee cup.

Bronwyn shook her head. "I've had enough of pandering to rich ladies' whims," she said lightly.

The subject was dropped like a hot potato. A few minutes later they left the restaurant and walked through the crisp clear night to the parking lot. For the first time in months Bronwyn felt a chill in the air, and her sudden shiver was an invitation for Joe to lace an arm around her shoulder. A cold little ball settled in her stomach. To jerk away from him would show insensitivity and childishness, but she really didn't want to be touched—not as a woman —by Joe.

His palm slid down her back as he opened the door to a sleek dark green Mercedes. Just for a moment he clasped her shoulders again, a hug of pure innocent affection, she wanted to believe. Yet she felt uneasy when the car door snapped closed in her ear, like the slam of a prison cell. The whimsical illusion did not amuse her. She was well aware that Joe was playing on her sympathies, dredging up their past ties and her every past interest, but she was just as aware that he was a sincerely troubled man who needed someone. Her, he would have her believe.

There was no coastal road that connected Daytona's beach to New Smyrna's, though the beaches geographically bordered on each other. Inland it was rather a long half hour of long black asphalt ribbon, bordered by a steady stretch of greenery on both sides. "I've been thinking about selling the house, finding something older. Less typically suburban, more country."

"Joe, you're trying too damned hard," she whispered unhappily, and then hesitated. "There must be . . . someone in your life. Someone who makes a difference."

"I haven't had a woman since Lorrie was ill." Yet again he immediately dropped that subject when he saw her face avert to the darkness. It was a long time before he spoke again, and they were nearly back to her cottage by that time. "None of them ever meant anything, Bron," he said slowly. "I know that doesn't excuse anything, but I never felt you wanted . . . it wouldn't happen again. You're real to me, Bronwyn; I didn't know how real until you left."

When he finally left her at the back door she went into the house, dropped off her shoes, skimmed off her stockings, and whistled for Gypsy as she headed out the front door. On the beach she simply ran until she was exhausted, her knife-pleated skirt swirling high above her thighs in the night's ocean breeze. She knew Joe would be back, that she hadn't made enough of an effort to discourage him. She hadn't known how. She believed that he had honestly changed and that he honestly believed he needed her . . . and the child that had been part of their lives . . . Confusion touched her and stuck. Did she owe him?

She returned to the house, raised her fingers to lock the door, and was suddenly aware that Austin had been there. The locks on both doors were different, a double latch hook added to the front and a steel double key lock on the back.

And when she wandered into the bedroom, the sheets were still rumpled . . . on both sides of the bed. She sat gingerly at the foot of the mattress, exhausted. He had been there in the evening, and found her gone. Guilt sped through her. She felt sorry for Joe, who really needed someone, but at the thought of a long lonely night ahead . . . it was Austin on her mind, Austin who stirred a real feeling of life inside her. Austin who had left her with another man that morning as if it couldn't have mattered less to him.

The visit came out of the blue, four days later, a shock of life in an otherwise gray sort of day.

"The thing is, I have to go for my allergy shots. It's fall, you know, and this morning when I woke up I could barely breathe. But Mr. Steele is working so hard and he's gone till the afternoon, and Carroll here, she keeps asking for you. So I thought I might at least ask. It would just be for an hour or so, give or take the wait in the doctor's office—"

"Take your time," Bronwyn said warmly, "and stop apologizing, Mary. Carroll and I will be perfectly fine."

Worriedly the older woman pressed a kiss on both cheeks of her charge. Five feet of wiry build straightened up again, with a pair of bright green eyes focused vibrantly on Bronwyn. "I never leave her, you know. Sometimes the urchin escapes—the ocean, Mr. Steele must have told you. I've a fear of the water, and I'm just too old to change. But except for that—"

Reading between the lines, Bronwyn said soothingly, "Mary, I had a little girl. Just Caro's age."

"Yes. Yes."

"I swim very well. Gypsy's been trained as a life saver."

"Yes."

Bronwyn smiled. "I love her," she whispered.

The older woman relaxed. "Well, you behave for Mrs. Harmon now, Caro—"

"Oh, I will," the redheaded little girl in a crisp green pinafore promised solemnly. When the door closed Carroll let out an exuberant cry and raced over to hug Gypsy, who responded by lapping lovingly at the child's cheek. "Let's go swimming, Bronwyn!"

"There's a big undertow today, honey. We'll find another idea or two."

The cheesecloth was six feet long and a foot and a half wide. Carroll held one end and Bronwyn the other; when a wave came in they pulled the cloth up on the shore side. In went the minnows by the dozens, flashing silver in the afternoon sun. They raced to a long flat pan already filled with salt water. In a half hour they had over a hundred of the tiny fish, and they both crouched over the pan, watching the silver flashes streak through the water. Carroll cried when they were let go, but not after the next round, when she understood it could be done again and again.

After that they dug up sand crabs, poked at shells, watched motionless when a graceful egret screamed as it landed yards from them, strutting the shore line arrogantly, showing off. Pocketfuls of shells were collected that glittered gold in the sunlight, and Carroll's high-pitched laughter echoed on the deserted beach, as infectious as life itself.

Out of breath and sandy, they finally returned to the cottage for a snack and drink, neither of them anxious for Mary's return. Bronwyn studied the child for a moment, and then stood up from the chair at the dining room table, motioning Carroll to come with her.

"What?"

"I want to show you something."

Bronwyn led the way to the spare room, half laughing at the child's expression as she took in the disarray of paints and canvases and easels, so different from the order and serenity of the rest of the house. "Now, where . . . ?" she said absently. She heard the knock on the door and glanced up, then back at Carroll. "Here, Caro." She motioned for the child to sit comfortably and handed her a series of small watercolors. "They're animals, love. I was thinking you might like one. There's one or two of Gypsy; I think I've got a baby rabbit in there . . . you see if there's one you like. I'll be right back."

Hurrying back out of the room, she collided in the hall with Austin. Startled, she felt warm hands steady her shoulders and stepped back. He was laughing, radiating a vibrant energy that charged through Bronwyn like a shock wave. "I understand you got landed with the monster."

"We've been having a great time." She hesitated, trying to gather her scrambled wits together. She'd expected Mary, not this blue-eyed man who altered nice, placid days with dynamite. "The locks, Austin," she remembered. "I didn't thank you—"

"And I see they weren't in use. I walked right in. Luckily you look so damned good today that I don't have the urge to yell at you. The phone'll be in tomorrow, Bronwyn, and in the meantime I haven't surfaced from a desk in five days and feel like stealing a few hours off. I have in mind taking you to a rifle range. Have you ever shot a gun?"

"I—no." Her wits refused to unscramble. She found herself staring at the unruly shock of hair that rested on his forehead, the way his khaki shirt stretched taut on his muscled chest. The curl of sheer sexual awareness was instant, potent, and distracting, and she was suddenly embarrassed to see a very slow smile curl his lips as he caught her staring at him.

He leaned over, resting both arms around her neck, lazily drawing her close. "I've been typing the book nights and in Orlando days, Bronwyn. Some research I had to

91

check up on. I didn't want to call until I actually had some time—"

"It's all right." Now.

"Bronwyn!" The child called from the spare room, and Bronwyn reluctantly divested herself of arms and that physical hold of his eyes. Six months of self-sufficiency, she scolded herself ruefully, and all he had to do was walk in. Backbone turned to butter, and there was no reason to believe the man felt anything more for her than chemistry. Volatile chemistry, but still . . .

Her mood altered abruptly when she walked into the spare room. Carroll had chosen a tern from the watercolors, but the child was no longer sitting on the floor. The drape on another canvas, a large one, had evidently proved too much temptation for a curious mind.

"Who is she, Bronwyn?" the child questioned.

"Her name was Lorrie, Carroll. She was my daughter."

The work was in oil, unfinished, painted nearly six months ago when she'd first come here. The child had fine blond hair and Bronwyn's own cocoa brown eyes. She'd stopped working on it when she'd captured what she felt she had to—the eager-to-please smile, the shy tilt of the head, the innocence and eagerness to find laughter in life. Beyond was a canvas still white. Unfinished, as a child was an unfinished work, Bronwyn thought fleetingly, but for the first time in a long time she could look at the painting with more joy than pain.

"But where is she now, Bronwyn?"

Austin's arms suddenly tucked around her waist, drew her back to his chest. She hadn't even heard him come into the room. "Carroll—"

She knew he was going to scold her. "It's all right," Bronwyn told him, and to Carroll, "She isn't alive anymore, Caro." She smiled reassuringly at the child's startled look. "She isn't far. I like to believe she's half in my heart and half in heaven. Both very good places to be."

92

The child nodded. "Did she like to play with blocks?"

"All the time."

"Did she like to swim?"

"Very much."

"Do you like her better than me?"

Austin's arms tightened around her, but Bronwyn's hand touched his, silencing. "You should know a four-year-old's made up of ten percent peanut butter and ninety percent questions," she chided lightly, and crouched down. "Caro, I liked Lorrie for her shyness; I like you because you're not at all shy. I liked Lorrie because she was sensitive and gentle. You, love, I like for your spunk. What counts is getting loved for yourself, not the more or less of it. Understand?"

She nodded. "But I would just rather you loved me more," she said simply.

"That, punkin," her father intervened, "is called jealousy. Something we'll discuss another time." In two strides he had the watercolors put back in a neat stack and his daughter wielded high, a greeting kiss that had been missed. "In the meantime, monster, you've had Bronwyn all afternoon, and now it's my turn. Go find Gypsy and keep her out of trouble."

The child appeared to like the option, scrambling out of her father's arms.

Austin's eyes were suddenly all over her, his earlier vibrancy gentled, compassionate. "I'm sorry, Bronwyn."

"It's all right. I really don't break anymore." She took a breath and expelled it, as if relieved that it really was true. "Really, though, I'm much more in a mood to discuss whatever research you were doing in Orlando," she said lightly.

He shook his head, glancing away, and his eyes rested on the unfinished canvas. "You really have an incredible gift, don't you?" He half frowned, studying a half-finished

93

oil she had on the easel, a pair of watercolors on the wall. "You've done all this in the last six months?"

"It's getting to be a warehouse in here," she agreed.

"Private? You'd rather I didn't look?"

She flicked back her hair a little nervously. "Well, not exactly—"

"Good, go change your clothes then, brown eyes."

"Change clothes?" she echoed vaguely.

"Boots, long pants, long shirt. Ugly, sweetheart. And that will be hard for you. But the target range is in scrub country."

"Austin . . ." But a moment later she was behind the closed door of her bedroom, pelting off clothes. She still wasn't sure if she really wanted him to look at her work. She'd never been near a gun, a definite measure of her lack of fascination with them. And as far as the required attire for this outing, Joe's idea of spending time with her invariably included an elegant dinner and her best clothes. With Austin she seemed destined to look forever her worst.

She felt off-balance—he was good at doing that to her. She didn't like it, but there was the strangest sense of exhilaration whenever he was close. Sexual, yes, but also like a dynamite of adrenaline had been pumped into her. And there was the protective curl of his arms when he thought she was hurting, thinking of her daughter.

They dropped the child off at Mary's and the two drove awhile in silence. For a second time Bronwyn was struck by the difference in men. Joe's car was a sleek Mercedes that was vacuumed daily. Austin had a little red MG that was nowhere near new, had to have two dolls, a wrench, and a sheath of papers tossed in the back to make room for her, and he never once offered to put up the top in deference to her hair.

And that exhilaration kept coming. The wind whipped like cool fingers at her bare throat and arms, twirling her hair in helpless disorder. The sun shone so warmly, she felt bathed in it. The car hugged every curve as if it loved a race. Austin kept looking at her, smiling. She kept looking back at him, smiling.

When he finally stopped the car, they seemed to be in the middle of nowhere, the highway deteriorated to a path, then to a lumpy crisscross of sand and scrub. She saw the target set up from where he parked; there were a handful of pick-up trucks and a dozen or so casually dressed men waiting their turn to use it. The occasional explosion of bullets echoed every few seconds or so, an echo that seemed to penetrate her whole being. She had no idea where they were.

She glanced at Austin as he pocketed the car key, before either of them got out of the car. He reached over swiftly, pressed a single warm hard kiss on her mouth. "You probably think I was callous enough to drag you all the way out here to bore you to death, didn't you?"

She shook her head, ridiculously disarmed by the single kiss.

"As it happens, we're here for you, Bronwyn, not for me. I've been working sixteen-hour days, and when I get to bed I still can't sleep, thinking of you."

"So you thought of guns," she offered obligingly. A viable alternative if ever she'd heard of one.

"No," he scolded her. "I thought of you alone in that bed. The trail of thought varied from ensuring you weren't alone in that bed, to ensuring that when you were alone you'd feel some ability to protect yourself. That's how guns came into it. Not that you should own or even like them. Just that you should always know something about what you're afraid of." He vaulted over the side and began pulling out the canvas-sheafed rifles from the back. "Besides, I didn't think you'd appreciate my walking into your house, tearing off your clothes, and pouncing on you. I thought you'd appreciate a little conversation first."

"I've always appreciated conversation," she quipped lightly, but her color was suddenly high.

"I don't know about that. I don't think you need candlelight and champagne to tell you how you feel. Or have you slept so much better than I have the last few nights?"

No. For just a moment their eyes met, and there was suddenly no laughter in his eyes. She wanted him; there was no shame in letting him see. She could feel his desire for her in the depth of his eyes, just as honest, just as intense. But there was something else. Loneliness? For the first time she felt the smallest hint of his own needs. He would never woo by candlelight; he didn't want a woman seduced. And she felt like telling him that no, not with him, she didn't need the polite conversations and the rules. . . .

"Austin . . ."

But he was already stalking off with those crazy guns, and she stared after him with a bemused expression. He turned around on a sudden pivot and stalked back to her. Taut emotions had been masked, replaced by a glare that came from nowhere. "You never impressed me as lazy, lady. Why the hell haven't you done something about those paintings of yours? You really want to spend the rest of your life on one long vacation?"

CHAPTER NINE

She felt like she'd been slapped, and she glared at his retreating figure. Evidently he simply expected her to just follow after he'd sliced neatly across all the emotional and philosophical and intellectual reasons she'd spent the last six months alone and served them up like a bowl of gruel. Of all the insensitive . . .

But Austin wasn't insensitive. He'd proven that in his lovemaking, in the way he treated his daughter, in the way he'd treated her the night she had been afraid. He was just annoyingly sane, grounded in life and living as if those were the only options worth taking. At that moment she disliked him intensely, and slammed the car door so hard that several men glanced back in her direction, but none of them Austin.

Her booted foot immediately sunk several inches into the ground. The rain from the night before had reduced any right the terrain might have had to be called a field. It was a bog, clear and simple. Horseflies were arguing low with mosquitoes; the brush was of the cactus type, with stinging nettles and other assorted sharp spiny branches.

She took a breath, glancing around her as she brushed her heavy hair behind her shoulders. At least she was dressed for the outing; it was no worse than the island. And no one could deny that it was an ideal practice spot: no self-respecting human could conceivably desire to live within miles of it. She debated momentarily whether she'd actually felt more unnerved by his so bluntly admitting his desire for her or because he'd judged her cottage life a too-long vacation.

"Bronwyn."

Again, the half-dozen men there glanced back at her. She looked back at them stubbornly as she started forward. There was one distant chuckle and a pair of deliberately silent leers. The age of women's liberation obviously hadn't reached this group yet. She saw it differently. Obviously this business of guns couldn't be too difficult; the only claim to ignominy the one had was a wad of Redman in his cheek.

As she approached, Austin motioned her to crouch down on her haunches as he was. There were three rifles, each protected by their canvas covers, on the ground. When she moved to help him unzip the covers, he brushed her hand away. "Not yet. First the lecture," he said grimly, and continued working with the zippers as he talked. "I'm totally opposed to the stereotype of the handgun kept in the bedside table for protection. Too often that gun can—and has been—used against the person it was supposed to protect. Particularly a woman who never really took the trouble to learn anything about the weapon. Still, like I told you, Bronwyn, I believe you should always know something about an enemy, whether it's a person or a thing. Now if it had been a burglar the other night, and he was armed, and you knew exactly what the weapon could or couldn't do, you might have been in a better position to protect yourself."

Their eyes met and she nodded, most unwillingly feeling a little of the hurt and anger fade. They really were here for her. "I really don't ever intend to own one," she admitted honestly. "But I do hear you, Austin. I never looked at it that way. And, yes, I'm even a little curious."

"That's what we're here for. These may be primarily

hunting weapons and a long way from handguns, but the same principles follow."

A thirty-minute lecture followed before she was even allowed to touch one. She was tested in detail to ensure she was paying attention, and inundated with use, purpose, care, and function of each rifle—sixteen-gauge, twenty-gauge, twenty-two-gauge. Safeties, sights, stock, firing pins, barrels. Why one had accuracy to only fifty feet; why one could hit a target a quarter mile away, and the effectiveness of each. "There're three rules you never break: You never point a gun at anyone, whether it's loaded or unloaded; you never touch a weapon when you're angry; and you never use one under the influence of any drug—and I mean caffeine, alcohol, medicine, any drug."

She would have been offended at his brusque, even patronizing gruffness if she hadn't recognized the respect he had for the rifles, a respect he was communicating to her. Intrigued with his knowledge and finding the whole subject more interesting than she'd bargained for, she sat cross-legged on the ground and ignored the mosquitoes and increased cramping in her legs.

"Okay," he said finally. "Do you want to shoot one or not?"

She looked up at him, surprised. "Of course I want to shoot one."

"It's not really necessary, you know. I just wanted you to understand—"

"Austin, you've done your absolute best to terrify me. Fine. I am terrified. I hate guns. Are you happy? But I'm not leaving here until I've at least tried shooting once," she said crisply.

He shook his head, grinning at her, the first slash of a smile she had had in nearly an hour. "Choose your poison."

"The sixteen-gauge."

He frowned. "That's not an easy gun for a woman, Bronwyn. You remember I told you—"

"Austin," she said determinedly, "I remember everything you told me. Do I have to give the lecture back verbatim?"

The rifle in her hands was incredibly heavy. She loaded it, doing exactly as he'd told her . . . exactly, rating a thoroughly masculine smile that irritated her. His approval was fine, but she didn't like being treated like a cream puff. She stood up and took her place with the other men waiting their turn. To her embarrassment, the others stepped aside, with mocking, but not totally unkind, deference to the only woman in their midst. Determined all the more to do the entire thing exactly right, she stepped up to the firing line established by a bale of hay.

Austin stepped behind her, all instructor again. "Put your hand here, Bronwyn. And you butt the gun directly against your shoulder, or you're going to feel a backlash that'll hurt like hell. Press it into your shoulder hard," he repeated.

But Austin suddenly didn't feel like an instructor when he was cradled behind her, the front of his thighs jutting into the back of hers. His smooth cheek grazed her own as he discussed the sight on the rifle. The only thing she really heard from the moment he'd touched her—and that was vague—was that there was potential for pain. Obviously she was not going to jam the heavy thing in her shoulder ahead of time if it was going to bolt back on her.

The weight of the gun was so heavy that her arms were nearly trembling with the effort to hold it steady. "Have you got it pressed good and firm against you?" he demanded. "Bronwyn, I told you about the sixteen-gauge—"

"Austin, I'm ready," she hissed impatiently.

In answer she felt an incredibly familiar, very tender pat on her buttocks before he moved back several feet. She suddenly felt more muddled than Jell-O.

She put it back together in her head, removed the safety, sighted, very unobtrusively readjusted the gun away from her shoulder, set her finger on the firing pin and one palm of her hand in the exact support position he'd taught her, and fired.

The explosion echoed in her ears like a ringing pain, but not nearly as much pain as finding her bottom colliding with the earth and the weight of the gun collapsing on top of her. Belatedly she realized that her shoulder hurt like absolute hell and there were stars in the sky in broad daylight. The other men, as interested as they had been before, politely looked away. They, at least, were kind. Austin striding toward her had a look in his eye as if he wanted to kill her.

She pushed her hands down to get the momentum to stand up, and found them immediately immersed in mud. Austin snatched up the rifle, set the safety, and without any sympathy at all reached around her breasts and arm-pits with one long arm and hauled her up. "If you've broken your shoulder, I'm going to damn well murder you," he growled. "Of all the irresponsible, stupid . . . when I told you over and over—"

She brushed her filthy hands on the seat of her jeans, which didn't seem to help much since she found the same mud there. Her legs were decidedly shaky, and she was just as furious as he was. "I listened to every single thing you said."

He strode off toward the jeep with the trio of rifles case-up as if they were marshmallows. "You *listened*," he grated, "but you didn't *obey*. What did you think this was, some kind of game?"

How did he know she hadn't put the gun flush to her shoulder? Which, though he didn't seem the least concerned, ached like someone had just pummeled it with a closed fist. She winced with the motion of walking, and then trailed behind him, still furious but almost equally upset because he was. Rather belatedly she glanced at the black leather seats in horror. "I can't very well get in," she said in a low voice.

"Why the hell not? You have in mind going back to the rifle range?"

"I may just. It may just be that the next time you see me with a gun I'll be able to outshoot you," she threw back furiously. "But as far as getting into the car, damn it, I happen to be rather awkwardly—"

"What? Turn around."

Fuming, she displayed the muddy seat of her jeans. To her surprise he burst out laughing, and came around to her side of the car with a rag from under his seat. "Give me that," she flared. "It was all your fault anyway. I knew exactly what to do and had every intention of doing it until you—"

He brushed her hands away, stroking her back with embarrassing familiarity. "Until I what?" he demanded impatiently.

He was done, the rag tossed on the seat for her to sit on, and both of them got in and were driving out before he repeated, "Until I what?"

She was staring distastefully at her grimy hands. The mud was caked under her fingernails. "Until you . . . patted me," she said disgustedly.

"Until I . . . ?" His hand covered his mouth in a failing schoolboy's attempt to wipe off a smile. "I thought I was doing a damn good job of coming across like a drill sergeant," he remarked in an injured tone.

"Austin," she said warningly.

"Does the shoulder hurt?"

"No," she answered, "not at all." And he would never know otherwise if it killed her.

The MG bounced raggedly until they hit the highway again. By then Bronwyn was astonished at herself. She could not remember the last time she had shouted at anyone. She was not actually sure she ever had. Thrown a few pillows in her time, on one singular occasion a china cup when no one was looking, but as far as really letting go with anyone, whether it was in anger or any other emotion . . .

She cast Austin several covert glances as they drove. Evidently he forgot his temper as quickly as it came over him, but she couldn't forget the murderous look he'd given her when she was flat on her back. Not exactly in your placid, easy-to-handle category, she decided ruefully. Downright volatile on occasion. He seemed to bring it out in her as well, as if every time they were together her nerves started clamoring for life. What happened to the nice quiet woman who relished silence and craved nothing but peace in her life?

To her surprise, instead of taking her home he stopped the car in front of his condominium. "Just go in and start a shower, Bronwyn. I'll take care of bringing back some clothes for you and feeding the dog. There's a rocket launch tonight that should be terrific from the beach."

She blinked, and then gingerly applied one hand to the door handle. "Try 'Would you like to watch it with me, Bronwyn?' " she corrected him, disgusted.

He chuckled. "Would you please like to watch it with me, brown eyes?"

"Yes. Thank you very much." She slammed the car door with her thigh, not wanting to get the car any filthier than she already had. "And you can bring me a little vial of comfrey from the top kitchen cupboard by the refrigerator, thank you," she added with equal stiffness.

"Comfrey," he repeated vaguely. "What the devil is comfrey?"

"Nothing interesting." It was an herb effective on the worst of bruising. She could hardly tell him without admitting that her shoulder was killing her.

"Everything about you interests me, Bronwyn," he

called after her as she made her way up to his place. She half turned, startled by the sudden intensity in his voice. In a moment the car had backed up and was out of sight.

The driftwood fire splashed up sparks, and Carroll's face across from it glowed. Behind the child the sky was beaded with evening stars just emerging with the sunset. Bronwyn watched, smiling, and then raised one sticky finger to lick it at the same time the child did with one of her own.

"I really think you two children have had enough," Austin said sternly from behind them.

Quick as a flash Bronwyn snatched the bag of marshmallows and tucked it beneath her knees, winking at Carroll as she did so. The child chortled with laughter at the conspiracy against her father. Bronwyn suddenly felt two strong hands curl at the sides of her neck. She looked up and backward, staring only inches from Austin's firm mouth and row of startling white teeth. "Just where is this space shot?" she murmured blandly. "I think you invented the whole thing just to cook hot dogs on the beach."

"It's in twenty minutes, brown eyes." His lips hovered lower. Unconsciously her own parted in anticipation, but the very instant his mouth touched hers she felt his hand slap playfully at her thighs. Seconds later he was packing the retrieved bag of marshmallows with the last of the picnic debris.

"Are we really going to let him get away with that?" she asked Carroll solemnly.

The child shook her head delightedly.

"One of you is unquestionably going to get a spanking if you keep this up," Austin warned, his back still turned from them. Bronwyn motioned for Carroll to follow her and in an instant was on her feet, kicking up sand as she launched herself at Austin's back. Pushed off-balance, he crashed down on one knee in the soft sand with a startled intake of breath, but not before he'd reached around and taken her with him.

Flat on her back, her eyes closed to well off the instant bubble of tears. She'd almost forgotten the shoulder. Wrenched anew, she felt hot pain through her arm. Austin had been teasing, not rough, and the tumble in sand would never normally have hurt her, but she scolded herself inwardly for not behaving like a twenty-eight-year-old instead of like a child. Since when had she ever acted so nutty? In spite of the aching throb she managed an effortful "Get the bottoms of his feet!" to Carroll so no one would know.

"What's wrong?" The nonsense was gone from his voice.

"Nothing." Rapidly she blinked open her eyes. "I just got sand in my eyes."

The child tickled her father's vulnerable bare feet, and being the kind of father he was, he laughed even as he studied Bronwyn's face with another searching look. She had a moment, lying still and flat, to recover and catch her breath. She was standing, deliberately smiling, when Austin called an absolutely final halt to the horseplay, toting Carroll upside down and shrieking delightedly to a blanket by the dying fire. It was not, all in all, so difficult to smile. He really was wonderful with the child.

In a minute he had "his women" installed on both sides of him, the three of them waiting for the countdown for the rocket launch. Actually it was a satellite launch, according to the transistor he had turned on.

Dusk was just settling over the ocean. The waves quieted, became gentle little laps that just slurped to the shore and came back. When Carroll sleepily shifted just a little away from her father's chest, Austin turned on his side to Bronwyn.

"Two choices, brown eyes. Do you want me to look at your shoulder here or up at the house?" he asked mildly.

105

"Austin, there is nothing to see."

They were his choice of clothes he'd brought back from her house, beginning with the white gauze blouse that he now was unbuttoning. The emerald pants had been in the very back of her closet because they fit too tightly. She'd threaded the green and navy scarf through as a belt, and since she virtually had no proper shoes for him to bring, she'd gone barefoot. The effect of the colors and the trailing scarf and swinging dark hair was a bit like a pirate, female-style, the exotic slant to her dark eyes emotive when his knuckles brushed against the upper swell of her breasts.

"I told you there was nothing to see," she said wryly.

"What have you got there?" he demanded, perplexed at the layer of gauze even as he was undoing it.

Her left hand readjusted the blouse fabric, for the bottom two buttons he distinctly had no need to undo. "Comfrey. It's an herb. When it's made into a tincture and dissolved in water it soaks up—"

"Swelling." Grimly he stared at the dark violet color in the curve of her shoulder. "All right." He drew her up to a sitting position. "Now try fibbing, Bronwyn, and see how fast you get taken to a doctor. Does this hurt?"

He ran his fingers probingly in the area around her collarbone. "No." Slowly he rotated her right arm. "Austin, this is silly. I just bruise easily." At his black look she amended her statement weakly, "No. It doesn't hurt."

Austin's fingers gently probed around her back. Her eyes lowered, Bronwyn, suddenly felt uncertainty wrench through her. Pain was the last thing on her mind when he touched her. And when she was with him, it felt like forever, like they'd both laid bare a few vulnerabilities years ago and they didn't have to pretend they were less than human now. So easy to be herself around him, so natural. She knew how she felt, but as far as Austin's

106

feelings, any attraction he felt for her, she was more puzzled. Perhaps that was exactly the same way he related to every woman he took up with.

"Does that hurt?"

"Yes," she murmured unhappily.

Exasperated, he lifted an eyebrow at her. He was no longer probing, just rebuttoning her blouse. "There's nothing broken. I can imagine it hurts like absolute hell. You fib very well," he said dryly.

A flare to the south suddenly burned in the night sky firecracker bright. The three watched silently as the satellite soared to the outer atmosphere. So fast, so bright, so fleeting—in twenty minutes it was simply another star, no different from the rest.

Is that how she was for him?

"I'll be back."

Austin carried his sleeping daughter up to Mary in the house while Bronwyn waited, brooding, staring at the black, endless ocean.

CHAPTER TEN

The sands were a mellow gold in the night. They walked a distance from each other, Bronwyn claiming the smooth easy walk of the damp shoreline and Austin the heavier hills and valleys of dry sand. With his head bent and his eyes unmoving, Austin seemed at first as preoccupied as she'd been, but when he glanced up to catch her eyes on him, he raised an arm.

Smiling then, Bronwyn took the few steps to reach him, and that arm curled under her hair and around her neck like the taking in of a lariat. If she'd felt uncertain before, her tension helplessly disappeared when he held her. She tried to match her gait to his at the same time he slowed his pace to hers; and they both ended up stumbling, half laughing. "One of us is clumsy," Austin whispered teasingly into her ear.

"I failed ballet in the third grade," Bronwyn admitted.

"Nonsense. You couldn't fail anything if you tried. Your teacher was probably demented."

She chuckled again, but she was warmed by his nonsense. They walked the rest of the distance in silence, both of them content. As her cottage came into view, Bronwyn automatically took a step in its direction, but Austin caught her at the wrist. "I'm not coming up with you, Bronwyn. Let's just walk a little farther. I've got a solid week ahead of being closeted with a typewriter, and the fresh air feels so good."

Bronwyn walked with him toward the privacy of the island. The night was blacker as they progressed from the last of the inhabited area, and in time there was nothing but that velvet darkness of ocean and sky. She kept her head down for a time. Knowing he wasn't coming in was knowing he didn't want to make love with her. Fine, said her brain, her pride, her twenty-eight years of moral upbringing. Fine. Her shoulder hurt, she was tired, and she was still afraid of going too fast.

But she didn't look up at him for fear he would see deeper than that. Beneath the surface was a fierce aching disappointment; her blood, told to still, would not, and her heart ordered to stop racing in anticipation of his touch refused to listen.

Unsettled, she thrust her hands into her pockets, her toes digging into the sand as they walked. Again Austin suddenly clasped her wrist to halt her, and then very gently he fingered the gauzy material at her throat. "That morning, Bronwyn . . . obviously you still have something to settle with that ex-husband of yours."

The subject seemed to come out of nowhere. "Not 'settle'," she qualified immediately. "The divorce was settled, Austin. There's no . . ." She groped to find words that were accurate. "I bore his child and he seems to be in trouble. It's not an issue of reviving a relationship that's over."

"To you."

"To me," she agreed.

"That's not where he's coming from."

She hesitated, staring down at the mound of moonlit sand at her feet. "No," she agreed quietly, and looked back up. The moonlight at his back silhouetted a dark man of powerfully lean build, a sexual image that tugged again at the waiting current in her bloodstream.

"I may want you like hell, Bronwyn. But it's not going to work this way for me."

Her hair fell in soft folds as she looked down again. "I

109

don't know what you want me to say," she murmured uncomfortably.

"That you know exactly what you want, Bronwyn." His voice was critical and harsh and impatient—and it hurt her.

"If you're asking if I know what I'm going to do about Joe—no, I don't know yet. If you're asking if I know what's going to happen between the two of us, Austin, no, I don't know. And I don't think you do either. But if you're asking how I feel right now, this minute, yes, I know what I want. But I think you're implying that that doesn't really matter." She turned on her heel, whipped her hair back from her cheeks, and started walking again toward home.

He was there like lightning, brushing the quick tears from her cheeks, bending to kiss them away. "It matters," he said huskily. Before she could draw breath, his smooth lips were hungrily covering hers, her hair whipping around both of them like a concealing curtain as a restless breeze started to blow. She heard a faint involuntary groan come from the back of his throat as he crushed her close to him, his earthy scent more potent than a drug. "But we're not going inside, Bronwyn."

She heard him. No matter how much he wanted her, he wouldn't play unless he was convinced she was absolutely free and clear of other commitments. It was to be just kisses, not beds. And here was safety, a public beach, neither of them the type or the age to tolerate interruptions—but there was no one there. No lights, no cars, and the island insects were humming a song of privacy.

She wanted so much to promise him she wouldn't see Joe again, but she couldn't do that. But there was no Joe between them, no matter what he thought, and she sought to convince him with her touch. Her right shoulder wouldn't give as she wished, but her left hand roamed a feverish pressure up and down the warm taut skin of his back, loving the supple give of muscled firmness. Her right hand moved more slowly, fingers splaying in the bristle of chest hair beneath his sweat shirt, catching it up in a fist and then loosening. The feel of his lips in the softness of her neck, the vibrant possessiveness of his palms cradling her closer—she needed this man. Right, wrong, fair, unfair. She needed his laughter, his anger, his sense of life, his . . . loving. She'd needed it for all her life.

"Bronwyn, cool down," he warned hoarsely. But, helplessly, her lips were ready for him again, and he was there, his tongue playing with hers, their familiar tastes mingling.

The sand was cooler than the night itself, like a rumpled blanket that yielded and shifted to accommodate her shape. His mouth never left hers as she seemed to sink lower and lower, and then for a moment she was lifted again as he removed her blouse and the night air caressed the white satin flesh. So close she saw his eyes just above hers, liquid dark, intense. Cool down, he'd said. That was no longer in his eyes. It had never been in hers. The chilling sand on her back contrasted to the languid heat of his mouth and tongue on her breasts. Her toes dug into the sand when she heard the zipper of the green pants. His mouth trailed the path from breasts to ribs to navel, to the smooth velvet skin just below her waistband.

"Austin . . ."

He crawled back up to claim her mouth again, his weight heavy, hard, demanding a yield from her own that was already crying willingness. The self-controlled woman who'd always worried about every word for fear of hurting someone—she wasn't that person. He was the only one who promised her every pulse, her every heartbeat, that what she needed herself was just as important. He praised the helpless murmurs in her throat, her restless groping for him, the strain she felt as her back arched, every limb reaching for him.

111

"Austin . . ."

"Damn it. Why the hell didn't you have the sense to go up there and lock yourself in when you had the chance?"

She laughed helplessly. They rolled in the sands, the surf pounding at their feet. At one point she felt the cold froth at her toes. Then her pants were gone, his. She felt his tongue teasing at the inside of her thighs, shocking her with its intimacy. He scolded her shyness, stroking her hair, fanning it to lay on the sand like a smooth black blanket around her moonlit face, around her dark eyes pleading up with him.

"No."

She heard him. He resented the loss of control in himself, and that he would risk her exposure. Yet the chances were all but nonexistent, on the island, at this time of year, at this time of night. His frustration she loved; his fierceness she drowned in. No one would dare come. She believed that. Every touch that incited him out of control she wanted to know, and like a fierce driving yearning inside of her she wanted to cleave, to hold, to join.

Slick with silky moisture, he towered over her, the moonlight part of the glaze in his eyes. She shifted her hips, her eyes open, love pulsing through her veins. He took the love offered. She wanted to give it. Nothing had ever seemed so simple in her entire life, so right, so free.

A bleary, boring drizzle snaked down the windows. Bronwyn, with her hair kerchiefed and a dustcloth in hand, found herself wandering into the shuttered spare room just to get away from the intrepid gray.

It was a difficult room to vacuum. For that matter it was an impossible room to clean. Canvases just seemed to have reproduced like rabbits. A half hour after she started she was kneeling on the carpet, distinctly not happy, looking through her work.

Laziness, Austin had accused her of.

She threaded through canvases, sketch pads, watercolors. A kind of joy had triumphed over grief in the painting of Lorrie the first weeks she had been here. That was the beginning. Then the island at dawn; the beach, rain washed; the soar of a gull; the humor of sandpipers at play; an old man, beachcombing. All emotions expressed, released, as she had never seemed to be able to do with people. The skills had begun with extensive art courses a long time ago; the sense of color was uniquely her own. She rarely pleased herself; she was too much of a perfectionist where her own work was concerned. Decisions that afternoon, then, didn't come easy.

She had style.

Unfortunately, she would prefer to give up eating over painting.

So do something with them, she told herself gruffly. *At least try. Say out loud that it's what you really want to do. Austin was right. Damned cruel, but right. You have been on one long vacation since Lorrie died.*

She changed clothes and braved the dull gray rain and Gypsy's protesting moans, filled the backseat of her car with her canvases, and headed for Daytona. There was a variety of galleries in Daytona; she'd been to all of them at one time or another.

She returned that night at seven, and the next night at seven, and the next night a little later. They were all painful experiences. She felt like she was exposing herself naked on a street when she exposed her paintings. The owner of the first gallery she tried, as it happened, had a stable of local artists and room for no more. Perhaps it was a rare moment of compassion—he'd at least agreed to look at one or two. Two now hung on his gallery walls. "Don't expect on them drawing any kind of price. It's not like you're known."

Two galleries took none; another six. Two craft shops took paintings on commission. She was told that paintings

113

were the last priority in this economy, that she had an incredibly fresh flair, that her animals were "darling" but her seascapes too emotional, that her seascapes were marvelous but her portraits too moody, that her portraits were outstanding but wouldn't sell because her subjects weren't "popularly attractive."

In spite of herself, exhilaration began to surge through her as she felt ambition stir again, a momentum to accomplish that she'd simply lost when Lorrie died.

It was little more than a week later that she was sitting in her living room with Gypsy in front of her. She was wearing an old frayed shirt and cutoffs and she was laughing. "Money!" she explained to the listening dog. "I know you can't understand, but it's the first money I've gotten— my way. Just completely for me!"

The dog obediently cocked her head. Bewildered, Gypsy was trying to make sense of a mistress who opened the mail and started dancing around like a mad thing.

"Look," Bronwyn insisted, waving the check in front of her.

The dog looked, leaned back, and scratched her ear.

"You have a terrible attitude," Bronwyn told her. "And no, I'm not going to call him. We both know I want to. We both know he's busy and that we don't really think that's a very good excuse for not calling. Besides, he was a bastard to goad me into this. Now, wasn't he?"

The dog again scratched at her ear.

"It's going to be a terrific letdown to have to give you a flea bath, do you know that? You don't seem to have any comprehension at all of how absolutely terrific I feel! People just don't sell paintings, just like that. It's a beginning. . . ."

The dog, loath to discuss finances, was immediately more interested in the subject of water in any form. A tub was dragged out in the front yard and filled with anti-flea

114

shampoo. There appeared some question who was the more soaked in a matter of minutes but Bronwyn was laughing, delighted at Gypsy's antics, and singing torch songs off-key in her sexiest voice for the benefit of no one. Gypsy fancied herself a singer as well. Whenever an ambulance siren went by she howled the melody. She seemed to think the same of Bronwyn's singing.

"Rinse time, you big bear! Sit still!"

She didn't know what made her suddenly turn toward the house, but she did. Joe, meticulously dressed in a cranberry linen suit, was watching her from the doorway, his blond hair brushed back and his eyes concealed by Foster Grants. "I knocked, Bron. You didn't hear me, so I—"

A hundred and forty pounds of wet fur launched herself from the tub, the growl instant and menacing.

"Gypsy!"

The dog halted and backed to Bronwyn. She took a step forward and so did the dog, determined to stay between her mistress and the man in the cranberry suit. "I'm sorry," Bronwyn said helplessly. "Gypsy!" she hissed furiously.

Joe was as pale as he was tight-lipped.

"If you'd try and make friends with her," Bronwyn suggested unhappily. "Joe, you must remind her of someone. She's always so gentle—"

"I've driven a hell of a long way, and you know I hate dogs, Bronwyn. If you wouldn't mind just coming in and locking that bear out—" He glared at the dog, who growled right back.

Bronwyn sighed. What was he doing here? In the house she found a marvelous bouquet of two dozen yellow roses, a box of chocolates, and a bottle of Joy, his favorite perfume on her and one she had frankly never liked. "Joe . . ." She flashed him a deeply unhappy look at the presents.

115

"Just give us a kiss to say thank-you." He sounded so suave, charming. But he looked damned nervous that the effect hadn't pleased her, and with his sunglasses off she saw deep dark circles under his eyes.

"Sure," she managed, adding swiftly, "but wait until I've changed clothes. I'll make you a drink—"

"Bourbon," he agreed.

It was a different restaurant he talked her into, darkly paneled, with anchors and fishnets and pirate's icons on the walls for decoration. The tablecloths were blood red and the waiters uniformed with eye patches. Candlelight glittered through the ruby wine in her glass when she raised it, and she noticed a single baked potato cost three dollars. What did they do, she wondered idly, grow them in Meissen china pots and beg them to take their fertilizer to justify that price?

Her hair was up, her makeup flawless, the dress an original that swirled crimson chiffon every time she raised her arm. She wore it because it was expected, because with Joe, as with her family, that was what came easiest. Not very happy with herself that evening, she tried desperately to recapture her earlier mood, telling him about her ventures in the art shops, about the check she'd received in the day's mail.

"But what does that represent?" Joe asked as he cut into his prime rib.

"Pardon?"

"Was that for one painting, Bron? Two? How much are you charging for each painting?"

She answered, but it wasn't the point to her. Still, she explained the price suggested by the gallery owners, their commissions, how they had suggested setting up a scale of prices.

When coffee was served, Joe said kindly, "Well, maybe it will work out for you, darling, but you certainly don't

116

have to be upset if it doesn't. That kind of money wouldn't exactly keep you in shoes for a year."

She didn't know exactly why or how it happened, but all of her exhilaration had faded by the time they were back in the car. Actually, Joe seemed to sincerely encourage her, smiling with enthusiasm for her "hobby," listening as he had rarely listened. Money had never been the point to her, but satisfaction and accomplishment, a concrete beginning to meeting her own creative needs in a productive way. But to Joe, productivity was always in terms of what it paid for. Everything he ever did had a purpose. And he was right, of course, from his viewpoint. On the way home, nursing a headache, it was just easier to listen than to try to talk.

"I have ideas, Bron. The management's old-fashioned; if Old Man Crouthers retires, I could be next in line. If I could just get my chance—"

"I'm sure you will," she reassured him.

"He's got this nephew. A nitpicky SOB. After you left I couldn't think. I admit I made some management mistakes. But that's all changed now that I'm seeing you again, and if they'd just really look now at what I've been doing . . ."

Alarm pulsed through her. Leave me out of it, she wanted to beg.

"You were such a wonderful hostess, Bron. If we had Crouthers over just once, I thought . . . He's an absolute ass on marriage and families; it might just be the push he needed—"

"Joe, I can't do that," Bronwyn said unhappily.

"Just once. One dinner. A few hours. Is that so much to ask?"

He sounded hurt, like a little boy.

She was silent, resentful of that.

He pulled into her driveway ten minutes later, turned the key on the engine, and sat there. A brooding, handsome profile he presented. "I lost Lorrie, too, Bronwyn," he said roughly. "She was ours, not just yours. I've had a hell of a time putting the pieces back together. I need help—I need you. Is one evening really too much to ask?"

The headache burgeoned like knife slivers in her temples. "No," she said lifelessly.

He smiled then. The charming smile she remembered well. "I'll give you a time and date," he said swiftly, and just as quickly changed the subject. "I never did get a thank-you kiss for the roses. Or is that something monumental—"

He made it sound ridiculous for her to object. Perhaps it was. She'd borne this man a child, and at one time she'd felt a deep and genuine affection for him, if not sheer sexual chemistry. She moved over swiftly to plant a kiss on his cheek. He moved too rapidly; their lips met instead, his arm going possessively around her.

It was dark, a melting silver sort of starry night. There was no one to see into the dark car. Certainly not Austin, if he'd even cared. Still, a dread pulsed through her veins, a panic of sheer don't-want-to. Joe's kisses were soft, gentle, damp. He meant to entice; there was no threat, no roughness, no fierce mind-searing loving as was Austin's way. She'd appreciated the gentleness.

She tried. He wanted her so badly to try. She endured the kiss and forced herself to return the pressure, but when his hand groped for her breast she felt a sour twist in the pit of her stomach that she simply couldn't help. She grabbed for his wandering hand, tried to simply press it warmly, as if to express affection, and bolted from the car.

Alone, Bronwyn leaned against the locked door and closed her eyes. She heard the car engine revving, and at last there was silence. She felt savage as she prepared for bed. Austin hadn't called. Twice she'd given him not just her body but a share in her soul. Joe at least wanted her, as a wife and—it would be stupid to deny it—as a bed mate. And he needed her. Austin didn't. Laughter and loving Austin took freely, but obviously he wanted nothing else or he could have picked up a telephone.

CHAPTER ELEVEN

The whir of the electric drill grated on Bronwyn's ears. Her perch was at best precarious on the lightweight aluminum ladder. Mildly cursing her lack of brawn, she finally had the trio of ceiling screws in place, followed by hooks, followed, with pleasure, by three ivory macrame hangers. Climbing down from the ladder, she wiped the moisture from her forehead absently with the sleeve of her shirt. It was a coolish day everywhere but that last twelve inches beneath the ceiling.

She had in mind a corner of greenery in the bedroom. A luxurious pair of dieffenbachia was already potted, and above them she wanted to hang three star of Bethlehems, loving their elusive sweet fragrance. It was all done now but the potting, and a few minutes later she was kneeling on the terrace with dirt, a spade, chips of brick, and three coral ceramic containers.

The phone, so recently installed, predictably didn't ring until she had her hands immersed in dirt. With a grimace she hurriedly raked her hands in the grass, whipped her hair back from her face, and half ran to the kitchen.

"Bronwyn? Have you got a few hours free?"

She flicked on the faucet with the phone cradled in her shoulder, trying to rinse her hands clean. After more than a week of silence, she thought vaguely, Austin deserved at least a measure of coolness. "I—yes."

"Fifteen minutes."

"God in heaven. A full thirty."

"Twenty, brown eyes."

He was there in twelve, an issue for which she would never forgive him. In a terry robe fresh from the shower she answered the door, a brush still furiously taming her hair, her feet bare. The plaster dust was still all over her bedroom and the hapless star of Bethlehems had been shoved into the pots, the mess still out on the terrace. Just once she'd like to see him when she was all put together.

"Austin . . ." she started irritably, and then looked at him.

"I know. I'll just get myself a glass of iced tea until you're ready. Don't scold, Bronwyn."

But the urge to scold had already died. Used to seeing him in jeans, Bronwyn was startled by him in business attire. The pale gray suit had a conservative cut and was paired with a light blue shirt. His broad shoulders suddenly looked broader, the blue eyes had picked up that gray like a hint of steel, and the set of his jaw reminded her of a man no one would want to bicker with. She didn't know where he'd just come from, but was quite certain she would have wanted to be sitting on his side of the table, not the opposition's.

More distracting than all of that, there was a white swath of gauze completely covering Austin's left hand, and beneath the aura of sheer male power was an odd, pinched looked around his eyes, a whiteness beneath his tan, and a distracted tension that radiated disgust.

Forgotten, very easily, were her own feelings. "Austin, what's wrong?" she asked gently.

"Nothing's wrong. Oh—I've spent the entire day in an accountant's office, and no matter how that kind of thing works out, I go stir crazy listening to numbers. And I've got work to do at home that I haven't been able to get to, but none of that's either here or there." He opened her refrigerator and pulled out a jug of sun tea, as if he knew it was waiting for him. His movements were stiff and

121

controlled, at total variance to the ease and economy of movement she was used to seeing. "I was going to drive out this afternoon to see some property I was looking at for my father. Not exactly exciting, Bronwyn, but the drive won't take us long and the weather's good for it. I thought maybe dinner after that . . ."

"Austin," she said patiently, "what happened to your hand?"

"Clumsiness."

He found a glass and poured his tea while she waited, and then shook her head wryly. Obviously that was the end of the explanation. For a moment she was willing to let that be, and she went into her bedroom still half carrying on a conversation with him. She hung up the terry robe and drew on silk panties and a slinky bit of rose bra, thinking that Austin looked like he needed any number of things, none of them a slinky bit of rose bra.

"How's the redhead?"

"Mary and Carroll are gone for a few days, as of this morning. She's got a granddaughter of about Caro's age; they've done a weekender on me before."

"Did you get those revisions done you were working on?"

There was a pause. "Not yet."

Of course. His hand.

The coral dress was light, open at the throat, and buttoned down the front to the hem. It was a breezy kind of dress; the gathered skirt flowed when she walked; the bodice had piping that accented the shape of her breasts. She felt good in it, and as she again brushed her hair in front of the mirror, she saw with satisfaction how the color accented her tan, and highlighted the same natural color in her cheeks and lips. After strapping on bone-colored sandals, she applied a light fragrance to her throat and wrists . . . and continually worried over the bandage on his hand.

She came back out to find Austin looking as if he'd half thrown himself into the chair, his head leaning back and the glass beside him empty. His eyes snapped open the moment she walked in, and some of that blend of exhaustion and tension seemed to leave his face, replaced by something much more relaxed and familiar. He started with her ankles, worked up the expanse of calf to skirt hem, trailed the road of buttons over feminine hills and valleys to her open throat, rested there on that pulse suddenly beating erotic rhythms. Up again over coral lips, the vibrant shine of coal-dark hair, the glow of honey complexion, and the sweep of lashes over cocoa-brown eyes. Back down to her toes, which were curling helplessly for the inspection.

"Stop that!"

"God, I'm glad you don't wear a lot of paint. Come here, so I can smell the perfume you're wearing."

"Austin—"

"Please."

She chuckled, but only approached close enough to take his empty glass. The desire was to touch and be touched—immediately. But other feminine instincts were just as powerful. "Could we possibly skip the drive and go right to dinner?" she coaxed. She had the feeling Austin had already pushed himself to the limits of his energy long before he came here.

"If you're in such a hurry," he drawled, "we could even skip dinner and go right on to more interesting pursuits."

Well, in theory they were on the same wave length, Bronwyn thought wryly. She took the glass to the kitchen, glancing covertly across the counter at him again. Distance helped. Her own theories were apt to get a little muddled up when they were in sexual-voltage territory. "You didn't get the revisions done because of your hand? Is it something you have to have done, Austin?"

"It was an issue of just wanting it done. I work within

123

a deadline, but I'm well within it. It'll wait," he said absently. He lurched up from the chair, and again she noted how exhausted he looked. Hurriedly she poured out a bowl of dog food, set it outside, and let Gypsy out at the same time. Coming back in, she closed and locked the glass sliding doors. Her mind was racing . . . worry, concern, the high she couldn't seem to control from just being with him no matter what shape he was in, an instinct urging her to be calm and careful and tactful.

He hooked her arm as they left the house, but she moved just a little ahead of him as they started walking down the drive. Without glancing at his hand, she said brightly, "Are you going to let me try out the MG or leave me forever wondering what it's like to drive a sports car?"

"Can you handle a clutch?"

"Nope."

"Hell." He handed her the keys.

She had a few moments to herself, while Austin changed out of his suit in the other room. Enough time to see dishes piled in the sink and a shirt strewn over a chair. Carroll's toys hadn't been picked up, and from a single glimpse through the open door to his office . . . well, there were bunched papers that hadn't made it to the overflowing wastebasket. A small thing like a bandaged hand hadn't evidently stopped him from trying to work. She had the fleeting intuition that Mary had taken Carroll away for the weekend because wounded lions could be impossible to live with, regardless of how gentle he was being with her.

"Stop that, Bronwyn." The words came from just behind her; she was squirting soap into the sink. She turned, grinning impishly as she surveyed the gray jeans and dark red shirt.

"Thank God. You're incredibly intimidating in a suit."

He moved in behind her, his right arm roping around

her waist to pull her back against him, his mouth nuzzling at the nape of her neck. "I've missed you," he whispered. "I know the place is a mess, brown eyes. Just sit down and I'll pour you a drink. It won't take me more than a minute to get it cleaned up."

"All right," she agreed. She turned the faucets on full, and added the dishes.

"Bronwyn—"

"I won't touch them," she agreed. One didn't argue with two-year-olds. "And in the meantime, I type about seven words a minute and charge a hundred a page. Are you going to show me your hand before or after you tell me what typing you need done?" She rinsed the dish in her hand and set it on the drainer to dry.

She glanced back. He was just standing there with that strange drawn look around his eyes that wrenched at her heart. She did love him. Like a whisper of freshness, just acknowledging it felt good. Which was not to say the immediate feeling was returned. He radiated thorough irritation; he really didn't want her doing his dishes, nor did he have much tolerance for being outmaneuvered, but in a moment that irritation seemed to give way to weariness. "I—your fee's a little high."

"But, then, you have no idea how good I am," she quipped and that, at least, rated an intimate smile. She could have absolutely killed him for letting the entire world fall around him before he let go of enough pride to ask for help.

"I have a *very* good idea how good you are," he countered, and watched the color mounting in her cheeks like steps on a ladder. Suddenly there was no smile. "No matter what it looks like, Bronwyn, I really didn't ask you over to do maid service. Or typing service. And rough week or no, I can still make you an excellent dinner."

She nodded. "Exactly. I told you once before that I don't do anything anymore unless there's something coming back. One steak in exchange for washing a dish or two. And I'm only jumping to type that stuff for you because of a disgustingly insatiable curiosity, so don't go jumping to conclusions about any higher motivations."

"Oh, yes, that selfish song. I heard the lyric one other night," he said dryly. "Only I happened to have been there the rest of that night. You just keep selfishly enjoying my dishes, brown eyes, and I'll do a quick fifty-two pick-up on the rest of the house."

After dinner she sat down at his desk in the study, going over the typing he needed done. Regardless of other motivations, she was intensely curious about his writing. Talking about himself didn't come easy to Austin, and by seeing his work she hoped to gain some insight into what made up the man he was.

He wasn't an easy man to know, she thought. Where he preferred old jeans and sweat shirts, his daughter's sunsuits had a Saks label. Where she knew a certain measure of success was important to him, he didn't seem the least interested in the outward signs of it; his comforts were all quiet ones and he was an intensely private man. He'd changed around a great deal of his life-style to accommodate his four-year-old, more than most single parents would have felt obligated to do. And though she'd been irritated with him more than once, the way he'd bulldozed her toward life again, she couldn't label him selfish. Not only that he'd waited for the invitation before making love, but his prodding her toward taking her own work seriously and that crazy trip to the shooting range . . .

You're digressing, she told herself sternly, and looked down at the stack of papers in her hand. There was an editorial mark he used that she didn't understand, so she got up from the desk and made her way back to the

126

kitchen, stopping soundlessly when she saw what he was doing.

There was a grimace on his white mouth as he peeled off the bandage, accompanied by a sudden pearl of sweat on his forehead. She caught only one glimpse of his palm before he sunk his hand into the water. One look was enough. She must have made a sound, because his head pivoted around, and she saw irritation in his eyes at being discovered. "I thought you'd be at least a half an hour."

"Exactly why haven't you had that stitched?" she said, furious, stepping in to grab at his wrist. He shook his hand free from her, spraying water on both of them, but not before she had a really good look at the swollen angry gash.

"It's perfectly clean. Everyone knows it just takes time to heal something on the hand."

"When did you get out of first grade—last year? There's something still in that—"

"Don't be ridiculous," he snapped. "I've soaked the damn thing over and over. There is nothing in it and if I hate anything in life it's a fuss over—"

"We're going to a doctor."

He took his hand from the water, carefully dried it, applied first aid cream, and rebandaged it. "Just listen, would you?"

"For a second and a half," she agreed.

He leaned back against the counter, and then, as if on second thought, turned around and brought down a bottle of Scotch from the cupboard. "I never told you how I learned about guns," he said casually. "My dad used to own a little fishing fleet off the Keys; we'd go into the Everglades on vacation. That was fine and good until I was about seventeen; then I decided I'd had it with that kind of life. I wanted more security than that offered. My mother looked ninety before she was forty; I didn't want that

127

for me or to inflict it on anyone I cared for. So I took off, as far as I could go. Alaska was stop one."

"Alaska," she echoed, unwillingly but momentarily distracted. So he was actually capable of talking about himself. She took the bottle from him with a speaking look, and poured water into his glass and some ice cubes. The kind of painkillers she had in mind for him just might not mix with alcohol.

"Alaska. Obviously you don't read Nick Slolan," he said dryly. "Anyway, I was a game-hunting guide—more than two years apprenticeship to earn that title, then a year and a half of earning it. Incredible country—caribou and elk, moose, bear, wild country like you've never imagined wild country, everything bigger than life. It was too damned lonely for an entire life of it, but for a while it suited me very well. The side of the coin that's immediately relevent, though, is that a guide is the one who has to cope with everything—avalanches, frostbite, broken legs, blizzards—"

She had a sudden glimpse of the real storyteller he must be, but more than that she considered he must be damned near desperate if he was suddenly so willing to talk about himself. "Tell me after I make the call to the doctor," she said firmly.

"I don't have a doctor, nor do I need one. Trust a woman to overreact," he snapped with biting sarcasm. "Mother Caro, Bronwyn; she needs it. I don't. There's only one thing I need from you—"

"Behave," she suggested, knowing he was about to hit below the belt.

"I have set two broken arms in my time," he barked. "It's only since just before Caro was born that I moved back here. I've been around. Would you believe I delivered a baby on the side of a country road in France, where there'd been a car accident. Sun blindness, one guy who had to be carried down one of those itty-bitty canyons in the Tetons—"

"Stop showing off," she chided him. "All those things happened to other people, obviously, not to you. There's never been any question in my mind that you were a man, Austin, so you can just take the rest of this macho monologue and shove it. I couldn't care less if you faint where your own blood's concerned, idiot!"

"I don't—" She stood absolutely still when he came toward her, stalking like some avenging, vibrant, menacing . . . His good arm went around her neck, gentle like cotton down. He dragged her close and held on. "I swear, I could hit you."

"Hmmm." Her arms went around his waist. She reached up to kiss his cheek. His threat didn't seem particularly impressive.

"Bronwyn. I didn't mean that. About the only thing I needed from you—"

She knew that.

"I told you it was nothing."

Bronwyn didn't bother to reply, trailing after Austin to the door of his condominium. He had had a quarter-inch sliver of glass deeply embedded in his palm. The wound had been cauterized, but not before he had been shot up with painkillers and antibiotics, and his eyes were now all pupils, a glaze of double vision that made it difficult for him to even fit the key into the lock.

She switched on the light and closed the door behind them, hurrying then to head him off before he could collapse in the living room, regardless of what he thought. She already had a full measure of how he'd spent the last few days, and very little of it had included sleeping. Between exhaustion and the drugs, his arm slung around her shoulders like dead weight in the darkened hall.

She managed to get him into his room. Moonlight haloed the king-size bed and the rich Oriental furnishings she'd only glimpsed once before. It was no little relief to deliver his heavy weight to the mattress. She knelt on the carpet to pull off his shoes.

"I'll do that." His voice was slurred, heavy. "For God's sake, Bronwyn, there's nothing wrong with me. You couldn't even see the damn little—"

Socks followed shoes; then she knelt on the huge bed next to him, dragging down the covers on the one side and readjusting the pillow. His hand circled her ankle, snaked slowly up her bare calf and she suddenly shivered, shifting away, half smiling in the darkness.

"Move up," she whispered. "Just to the pillow, Austin."

He managed that and she knelt over him again, brushing her hair back from her shoulders, and unloosened the buttons of his shirt one by one. Almost unconsciously her fingertips traced the golden skin of his chest as she pushed the material off. She could hear his breathing and then he was flat on his back again. Silently she unbuttoned his jeans and unzipped them. Suddenly she felt his hand cover hers.

"Aren't you . . . aggressive?" the sleepy voice whispered.

He was asleep, this time for good, long before she'd framed an answer. The teasing whisper echoed, though, as she worked to tug off the jeans, as she shifted him enough to reclaim the sheet, as she covered him to the chin, covered his physical arousal to her touch. But arousal was an instinct, not love.

She got off the bed, switched off the light, and stood staring at him for a few moments in the darkness before she left the room. She couldn't stop thinking that he'd waited a very long time to call her, and then it had taken a fever. He didn't want to need anyone—even her.

CHAPTER TWELVE

Bronwyn stood in the middle of the dark living room absently rubbing a weary hand at the nape of her neck. So what did she do now, stay or go? Go, obviously. Sleep was what he needed and the painkillers would ensure that; in the morning he was going to be nursing a sore hand, but he would be fine. In a weak moment perhaps he had allowed a bit of caretaking, but she had no illusions he would appreciate, want, or tolerate that sort of thing when he was himself again.

Go home, she told herself, *and worry all night that he'll need someone when the painkillers do wear off.* Not particularly comfortable with the decision, she took off her shoes, tossed one of Austin's sweaters over her shoulders, and stretched out on his rust-colored couch in the living room. But sleep proved elusive even though she was exhausted, and she found herself wide-eyed, staring at the moonlight weaving silver patterns on the carpet. She kept thinking. That was the problem. All the travels he'd been on, all the things he'd done. In contrast her own life seemed remarkably sheltered; even the tremendous momentum it had taken for her to break away from the old patterns of her life seemed like nothing next to the kind of crises Austin had dealt with.

When the wanderlust had left him, he'd decided to settle down, with an adventurous woman probably much like himself. That woman had failed him, and he had a daughter whom he obviously loved fiercely. The two were a tango all their own. Did such a self-sufficient man really need anyone else beyond someone to satisfy a sexual need?

His weakness touched her, his unforgivable and utterly ridiculous fear of doctors. She knew of no other weaknesses he had. She felt like clinging to it, just as unforgivably, just as ridiculously. He had needed her. It was the only arena where he'd specifically needed her, where any other woman with a reasonably attractive face might not have done.

At two in the morning he stumbled out into the dark room and stared at her still figure on the couch. His tousled hair caught the moonlight; his shoulders captured it in a silvery ripple as he bent over her. "What are you doing out here? Why on earth haven't you come to bed?" he demanded in a husky whisper.

It seemed he was the one who was fully awake this time and she was sleepy. He took her hand and then pulled her to the curve of his shoulder as he led her through the darkness to his room. With his head bent to hers, he tried, one-handed, to unbutton her dress.

"Look. Austin . . ."

"You can't sleep in your clothes." He managed the buttons and belt. Her dress made a strange wooshing sound as it fell to the floor. Then there was no sound inside the room. His open window allowed in a cool salty breeze; the ocean was pounding out its rhythms. She was silent, feeling his eyes, as sensual as his touch itself. Her lingerie looked like satin by moonlight, and her figure was softly and explicitly shadowed against the sultry darkness of her long hair.

"How does your hand feel?" she asked helplessly.

"Do you want an apology for my behaving like a perfectly bloody bastard?"

She half smiled, shaking her head no.

132

"I did call you last week," he said quietly. "You were out. I guessed with your ex-husband."

She had taken walks many of those nights. He might have called on any of those occasions, not just the single time she had gone to dinner with Joe. "Don't make something of that that isn't," she said, her voice low, unhappy. "I told you, Austin, I don't feel anything for Joe anymore."

With a yawn he bent and rubbed his lips in the curl of her neck, draping his arms around her. The kiss was not sexual, but warm, affectionate, sensual. She could feel the tension from the entire day and evening fade, a wonderful sense of weakness slowly invading her limbs in its place. She kissed him back, and when they both got into bed he drew the covers close around their necks, cradling her close, pressing another warm sleepy kiss on her forehead. "You do what you have to do, brown eyes," he told her gently.

He was asleep before she was, and although she was disturbed by his soft words, her eyes closed not long afterward. In those few moments of half wakefulness, cradled so warm and close, she could not help but be aware that lovemaking had not been suggested, but she suspected that neither his injured hand nor any drugs would have stopped him if he hadn't guessed she had been out with Joe.

By ten the next morning Bronwyn was alone in Austin's study, reams of blank paper on one side of the desk and corrected copy on the other. For a solid hour she had typed, but for the last fifteen minutes she had her chin firmly ensconced in one palm, turning the pages over one by one as she read them. When she heard a door slam in another part of the condominium, she quickly shifted the pages back together, rolled a clean sheet rapidly into the typewriter platen, and pecked forward at a deliberate

133

pace. Austin's face peered through the open doorway. "You want coffee, Bronwyn?"

"No." Her answer was abrupt and annoyed.

"Fresh doughnuts?"

"No. Thank you," she offered belatedly, and then just as bluntly, "Go away, Austin."

Her typing skills had been reasonable in high school, but she hadn't used them since. Still, he had a marvelous electric typewriter that was willing to correct its own mistakes, and once she'd established a rhythm, her fingers fairly skimmed across the keys.

At two he came in, pulled the plug on the typewriter, and announced that crabs in the shell were going to be eaten in the dining room for lunch. Most unwillingly she surfaced long enough for that, and long enough to see that he looked a thousand times better than he had the night before. Though she had to crack the crab shells for him, she could see his hand was not causing him near as much discomfort, that his temper was more even, and that he was starkly attractive in a velour pullover and soft tan pants that were for once not jeans. A shower had added a luster to his hair and his eyes were bright. He watched her continually throughout lunch, as if he weren't certain whether he was amused or annoyed at her obvious preoccupation with his work. "Are you finding it hard going?" he asked.

She shook her head. "But you obviously failed spelling in the second grade."

"I never meant for you to keep at it all day. I told you it wasn't that much of a rush, Bronwyn."

"I'll be done in two more hours, and then if you don't mind I'll take home the whole thing to proofread tonight," she said firmly.

His eyebrows rose at the oddly assertive tone in her voice, and then he leaned forward with a perplexed frown.

134

"Look, honey, I told you I wasn't Pulitzer-prize material. If for some reason the story is actually bothering you—"

It was, badly. "It's excellent and you know it," she said shortly.

At five she'd finished the actual typing, waved off an offer for dinner, and walked the beach home for the exercise with the manuscript in her arms. Gypsy had to have her quota of attention and some sort of snack had to be eaten, but soon after that Bronwyn had changed clothes to a caftan and, barefoot, settled herself on the couch with the story.

The adventure was set in Alaska, a group of men hunting for caribou and black bear in the late summer—just a bit too late to be safe for Alaska's harsh climate. There was a woman along, of course, the redheaded wife of one of the hunters. The guide was the hero.

Austin had a way of searing into his characters like he would treat an apple; peel off the pretty outer layers and then gut. The naked fruit was served up to the reader, and his style was not wholly comfortable to her. In many ways the guide wasn't Austin—the hero had brown hair, was tall and very thin; he came from a wealthy family in the north. But in other ways . . .

Absorbed, she turned the pages. Action and danger were Austin's skills and there was plenty of it. Through each incident the guide showed an almost reckless disregard for his own life in contrast to a marked protectiveness for the others. Bravery was not the value placed on his actions, but a sheer don't-give-a-damn if he lived or died beyond the safekeeping of the people in his care. Cynical and brusque, a man's man, the guide took every risk there was to take, just barely making it out of each adventure alive with his skin intact. The wife of the hunter pursued him. He ignored her. The attraction was there, but he denied it. A desperation was part of him, an insidious loneliness that Bronwyn could ache for as she read; like

135

a man lost, he kept testing himself for answers to silent questions within himself.

The redhead succeeded in seducing him three quarters of the way through the book. The sex scene was torrid and explosive and burned Bronwyn to the roots of her hair; it was so explicit, so sexual. Angry with himself that he had taken another man's woman, the guide takes a lonely retreat for a day, leaving the others. He returns to tragedy —the woman's husband, selfish brute though he was, has died in a foolhardly confrontation with a black bear. The woman appears; the reader anticipates that they are both now free to pursue the relationship . . . in time.

Bronwyn set down the last page at three in the morning, feeling unsettled and disturbed and totally wide awake. The love scene played itself over and over in her mind. The woman was a redhead, a very long way from her own coloring. And Austin had had a redhead for a wife.

It was supposed to be a happy ending—a mixed blend of emotions, of course, as life was, but the husband had clearly been depicted as a creep, she thought wryly. But her own small smile didn't last. It didn't feel like a happy ending to her. The guide was seduced into taking another man's wife; he had not resolved that, in the end. And she thought that the hero had felt obligated to take the woman on, with her husband dead and the woman alone in the wilderness, rather than the free-to-love-now ending that the story implied.

You are an expert at wishful thinking, Bronwyn, she told herself idly as she rubbed wearily at her temples. *You just don't want to believe he loved his wife or could still love her, because you love him yourself.* For a moment she silently tested her feelings for Austin. It was the second time she'd done it, and there was really no surprise that *love* and *Austin* coupled in her mind.

It was late. She got off the couch with a long stretch for limbs that had been in one position for too long. The doors were already locked, but she took her teacup to the kitchen to rinse out, and then starting turning off the lamps, wandering finally back into her bedroom. It was pitch dark within, a moonless night, and the echo of waves sounded troubled outside. She felt troubled within. Austin's feelings for her . . . she didn't know. But she had a glimpse of understanding why he reacted in certain ways to Joe. Did Austin, could he, love her? Would it make a difference to him if she never saw Joe again?

But she could not do that to Joe, not for those reasons. For however indifferently he had treated her during their marriage, there were still and would always be certain ties. Not just their daughter and her death. But no one could erase eight years and pretend another person just didn't exist, particularly when he was in trouble. That last business dinner she had promised . . . She would help him for that singular occasion, but then she was going to make it absolutely clear that that was all.

She was curled in a totally contented ball when she heard a rap on her window. Her eyes blinked open to a pearl-gray haze of pre-dawn light, and sleepily she closed them again. The sound was repeated on the glass doors to her bedroom, and finally, reluctantly, she sat up, glancing at the alarm clock. Five o'clock. With a sudden shiver of alarm she leaped from the bed, hurrying to the curtain to part it wide enough to see her visitor.

Austin was wearing hiking boots, khaki pants, and a tan safari jacket. Above that were a pair of dancing blue eyes as wide awake as hers were distinctly not. He motioned at her to open the door, and brushing her tousled hair back sleepily from her forehead, she did. "What on earth are you—"

"Don't you ever open the door again dressed like that, brown eyes." He bent to kiss her sleep-warmed lips.

"You just told me to open the door," she protested

137

groggily, and then flushed, snatching up her silk robe from the floor where it had fallen.

"You always sleep like that, do you?"

"Usually I like a pretty nightgown. Only when I'm expecting visitors in the morning . . ." She quipped, teasing. Her smile was radiant. Seeing him was a bit like letting in a cyclone at this time of the morning, but she happened to be in love with his particular brand of storm.

"Why didn't the dog at least bark? Does she let just anyone in anytime?"

"You surely didn't come here to start harassing me before I was awake?" But she thought, fleetingly, of the different reception Joe got every time he was within yards of the dog.

"Of course not. I figured you were going to sleep all morning."

"All morning?" She motioned expressively to the clock.

"Time for a walk. Get dressed before I change my mind completely about the morning's activities." His eyes suddenly glinted the options, but not for long.

He allotted five minutes for teeth-brushing and dressing and another five for a cup of tea and a banana. She was ordered into hiking boots and long-sleeve shirt, and when they were outside he pushed a cap rakishly on her barely brushed hair. Ruefully she only shook her head at him. She hadn't even had time to put on lipstick, and she had no illusions the cap added anything in the way of glamor.

"You have a specific walk in mind?"

He nodded, striding ahead of her. "Ducks. It's that time of year and that time of morning."

Rose hues slowly filtered over the ocean as they walked, the sea reflecting the sky's colors like a mirror. Pastels played at the horizon, turning from pinks to violets, then orange as the ball of sun perched on the water, resting before its days ascent in the sky. The waves hit at the shoreline, all but still, the low tide leaving a long expanse of silent white beach. She loved it, the sunrise, the silence, his warm firm hand in hers.

When the color show was over, they crossed over the beach to the barrier dune, pausing to watch a raccoon feed on the abundance of seagrapes that populated that area, both of them smiling at his greed. The terrain was sandy and marshy, not easy walking, but, then, neither of them were in a hurry. Gulls and terns were busy overhead, fetching breakfast from the waters and hauling it back to the brush to feed on in safety. Herons, egrets, sandpipers, they saw, and then a single slow green sea turtle. The birds were full of conversation, singing, scolding, cackling their morning gossip.

She pressed closer to Austin as they traveled a thicket of saw palmettos on their way down to the lagoon side. The huge fan-shaped leaves less than a month before had spawned a profusion of tiny white fragrant flowers. Bronwyn had stopped then, and discovered both a mouse and the vividly marked pine snake that was stalking it. Austin stuck his hand in her back pocket, pulling her close to him. "So you know about those, do you? But they'd a hundred times rather have a rat or mouse than you, as attractive as you are," he whispered teasingly.

"That's very nice. I even believe you. Just as long as you understand that if we come across a snake, I'm going to jump on your shoulders," she hissed back.

He chuckled, his eyes only inches from hers. There was no reason to be whispering, except that the morning simply invited quiet. Just as she forgot totally about the saw palmettos and snakes, Austin's smile gradually faded as he looked at her dark-eyed, fragile beauty, her lustrous complexion, sun-warmed now, her lips already parted. Her arms went around him when he kissed her, dipping deeply into her sweet-tasting mouth, hungrily drawing her close. The cap slipped to the ground and her hair shivered free, and when his fingers moved to smooth it back, they stayed

139

there, splaying in the rich dark silkiness. The most primitive response stirred within her, as primitive as the landscape around them, the yearning a mixed blend of fierce and soft. He drew back and looked at her. She was no longer smiling, and neither was he.

"I thought we were going to look at ducks."

"We are," she said agreeably.

"Ducks don't seem to have any more appeal."

But they did, actually. On the other side of the barrier dune was a climb down to the roadway; another walk and they were near the waters of Mosquito Lagoon. Silently and slowly they both walked, and it was worth the effort. Hundreds, perhaps thousands, of ducks came to rest in the fall in the waters around the island. A few skittered nervously away when they came close, but when they sat silently on the low brush of the shore, the ducks came back, some to scold, some to check out the strange-looking beings. The pintails were the loveliest, their black and white coloring stark and sharp on their backs, their long tails graceful as they bobbed up and down for their breakfast fish.

After a time Austin stood up and took her arm again as they wandered back toward home. They spoke very little; they didn't seem to need conversation. At her cottage she invited him in, but he shook his head. "I've got that manuscript to send off—if you didn't find a ton of errors I'd missed?"

She shook her head, wanting to compliment him on his book but hesitating. In time. Just now she didn't want to think too much about what possible relation his characters had to his own life. If and when he wanted to bring it up himself . . . She brought him his book, ridiculously unhappy that he couldn't stay. "Austin, I—contacted some people about my paintings," she offered hesitantly.

"Of course you did. And were successful." He snatched at the cap and put it on his own head, then reached toward her to rearrange her tousled hair behind her ears. His lazy grin said that he liked it like that, and the tone in his voice told her that there had never been any doubt she would eventually come out of her hermit's shell, though she wondered if she ever would have if it hadn't been for him. "I have this silly urge to take you to dinner," he murmured as he bent to kiss her good-bye. "Actually go to someplace very nice, when I know darn well I'd rather see you without paint on your face or the kind of clothes designed to hide too much."

"I clean up remarkably well," she promised him.

"And maybe I'm afraid of that too. Thursday night?"

She nodded, a radiant smile of anticipation that slowly faded. "Austin, I can't Thursday. Any other time—"

He had too good an idea of her normal social schedule. "Your ex-husband?"

"It's only a business dinner, and it will be the last—"

"Fine," he said brusquely. "We'll just make it another time then."

But his eyelashes came down like shutters and his jaw tightened with a hard look. There was no other day suggested, nor any more kisses to add to their shared morning. Feeling perfectly wretched, Bronwyn watched him stride down the steps and out of sight down the beach.

CHAPTER THIRTEEN

"I hear you, Joe, but there are reasons why I've changed my mind. . . ."

"You can't change your mind now. Come on, Bron, we've got thirty people coming! I talked to your father, so we could use the beach house, and all the arrangements are made. I've hired the caterers, all you have to do is look good and hostess."

Bronwyn closed her eyes, cradling the telephone receiver between her ear and shoulder. "Joe," she said quietly, "since when has a dinner with 'just your boss' turned into thirty people? I thought this was to be strictly business—"

"It is. That's exactly why it's so important that you be there."

"And I can't even imagine why you brought my father into this."

"He knows Crouthers from way back. I thought you'd be pleased," Joe said petulantly. "The beach house couldn't be more ideal for a party, and then there's no two-hour drive to get you into Orlando and back. I did it just for you, darling, to make it as convenient as I possibly could."

Bronwyn hung up the phone a few minutes later, feeling a cobweb laced around her, tight and sticky. She heard, and did not want to believe, that a business dinner had been converted into a catered party, that her father had been brought into it, and through Joe's pleading voice and obvious sincerity she felt manipulated.

A great many of Joe's actions suddenly felt like manipulation. His coming so soon after her father's visit. The cultivating of old times with flowers and candlelight when Joe wanted a promotion, and when her father knew his boss. He'd promised no pressure at that first dinner and handed out more than a fistful of it. And he'd handed out a lot of promises a long time ago, all of them just as sweet as they were expedient—for him.

But the sincere quality in his voice, and the haggard look, and the circles under his eyes—those weren't lies. Her mind suddenly felt like a roller-coaster ride. She closed her eyes and thought of Austin. Do what you have to do, he'd said. And to trust her own instincts was what she'd tried to teach herself these last months, something she'd never done, always trusting others more than herself. The confusion cleared. As wary as she suddenly felt of Joe, and her sympathies for him were rapidly disappearing, she needed to know in her heart that she'd paid every debt, closed every chapter.

But when she thought of Austin she knew she was treading a very fine line, if she hadn't already crossed it. And she was suddenly desperate to have this dinner over with.

The dress was gold raw silk, clasped with a topaz on one shoulder and flowing loosely to her ankles. Her hair was swept back from the face with a riot of curls in back, her makeup expensive and flawless, although the wind tried to whip up all that careful perfection as the two hurried to the beach house. It was a wicked night, black and starless, with clouds hanging low and heavy and the surf angrily pounding the shore in the distance.

Inside the house Bronwyn caught her breath, giving her cashmere wrap to Joe. She had spent half of her childhood here, and "beach house" was a ridiculous misnomer; it was more a little palace that by accident happened to be on the ocean. It was a six-bedroom house with a pair of kitchens and a living room on each floor; the carpet was two inches thick and stark white throughout. Her mother loved white and gold and her father the old masters; original oils were in every room and the blend of priceless antique furnishings had never seen a wet bathing suit. It was as beautiful a place as it was untouchable. And the look of the place struck Bronwyn forcefully of how much her values had changed in the last few months.

The caterers were already there, preparing a seafood buffet—lobster, frog legs, caviar, crab. Champagne bars were set up upstairs and down.

"It looks just perfect. Particularly when you told me what a homebody sort of person your boss is," Bronwyn echoed back ironically to Joe.

"I just want to be sure he enjoys himself," Joe defended. "Come on, Bron. Enjoy yourself. I promise you it'll be a good party. Just be yourself."

"Myself is an old pair of jeans and a T-shirt, Joe," she said dryly. "You want me to change?"

"You're not even trying to be in a good mood," he said petulantly. "Bron, I need Crouthers. From the time I broke away from my father. I need my chance, and this is it. I need you. I can't do it alone."

At the taut, unhappy expression on his normally handsome features, Bronwyn felt a flash of guilt. "I'm sorry, Joe," she said quietly. "I am willing to help you; I just want you to understand that I'm not willing to—"

"We've been through that."

The doorbell rang and the flood of guests began. Bronwyn had been through it all before; the role was easy. Look interested. Be charming. Keep the drinks flowing. Pluck out the wallflowers; intercept the noisemakers with quieter conversation. Pretend that everything made her laugh. She tried hard for Joe's sake.

She cornered Roland Crouthers, a big, florid man, a mix of shrewd-with-men and gentle-with-women in the old-fashioned chauvinistic style. She liked him, actually. Joe had split up with her from the start, was circling the women as he'd always done at a party. She watched from the corners of her eyes. His white suit jacket was open and his champagne glass often raised; his tall blond looks were accented by a pair of sexy blue eyes and a deep tan. Where once she would have been deeply disturbed by his skilled flirting, she seemed to see it differently tonight. As rather sad, actually, as if he were not secure enough within himself unless every woman fell for him.

"Mrs. Harmon." One of the black-suited waiters tapped her on the shoulder. "We're ready to serve, if you . . ."

It was not too soon for dinner. The champagne had been flowing just a little too freely; the group seemed to be having a good time. But there was a restlessness, perhaps a precursor of the storm that seemed to be building outside. The beautifully landscaped gardens could not be used because of the wind, and clustered within, the smoke and champagne scents mingled in a cloud.

Once dinner was over, Crouthers and Joe closeted themselves in a corner, a champagne-oriented corner, but Bronwyn was pleased. She heard pleasant bursts of laughter that indicated they were getting along well. She wandered from group to group; she knew some of the people, she'd at least heard of each one by name. She was laughing at a joke when she half turned to see two latecomers enter the room. Her father and mother. Her jaw dropped and a strange feeling of unease troubled her as she hurried over to greet her parents. "Of all the people I didn't expect to see tonight . . ."

She bent to kiss the soft, perfumed cheek of her mother.

Mild in looks and soft in manner, Marianne was short, very pretty in an unobtrusive way, and had been led all her life by her domineering husband. Theodore came first in her life, not that Bronwyn had ever felt unwanted. More, she had been confused when she was younger; a woman's happiness was in being subordinate, her mother's life told her, and when Bronwyn had been unable to find that same sort of serenity in her own life, she felt she was the one who was lacking.

"You look lovely, darling," her mother said warmly. "We just had to come! I knew Joe could bring you out of seclusion, and right here at home really. This house has so many wonderful memories for all of us! Doesn't it feel good to be out with people again, sweetheart?"

"I . . ." Her father stepped ahead, and bent to kiss her as well. English Leather wafted around her like another of those cobwebby feelings.

"Take care of your mother, Bronwyn. I'll go see if I can help a few things along for Joe." With an eagle's eye, her father had already spotted the two in the corner.

"Did you stop for dinner on the drive?" Bronwyn asked her mother. "We've just finished, but I'm sure I could get you something—"

"Well, a little something then, dear."

Bronwyn hurried off, and when she returned with a plate and drink for her mother her mind was spinning. *I knew Joe could bring you out of seclusion.* What had he told them?

She listened to Marianne's local gossip with half an ear, keeping a hostess's eye on the rest of her guests. More than ever, she simply wished the evening were over; she felt a sense of fraying nerves inside that she hadn't had in months, even as she was just as determined that nothing would go wrong with the evening for Joe.

By eleven she was exhausted, and the two glasses of champagne she'd had were floating in her bloodstream, a

146

sensation that she'd never particularly appreciated. Her mother had come and gone and was no longer glued to her side, and the best she could say was that the party was not only going well but would surely be over soon. At that moment it was rather loud, the air thick from smoke, and Joe was almost bleary-eyed from all the alcohol he'd consumed, his laughter carefree and his gregarious-host theme one he reveled in. He stopped to press an unexpected kiss on Bronwyn's cheek just as Roland Crouthers raised a hand in the center of the crowd for attention.

"I have an announcement to make." Crouthers lifted his glass high, gently tapping it with a spoon to quiet the crowd. "Most of you know I plan to retire at the end of the year. This seems as good a night as any to make it official, and to make something else official as well. Citro's had a hell of a time during this recession, and we're hardly alone as far as that's concerned. Though we've made it, and are going to continue to make it, the key very definitely is young talent, young ambitions, young ideas . . . and one man in particular, I know, has all the potential of really filling that president's chair—Joe Harmon. Come here, Joe!"

Joe flushed with pleasure, straightened his tie, and flushed all over again with pride. Bronwyn warmed for him, for his goal achieved.

Marianne, next to her, nudged at her shoulder. "He's worked so hard since Lorrie died, Bronwyn. You have no idea how much he's changed. I know it's going to be different for the two of you this time."

"Pardon?" Bronwyn turned wide eyes to her mother at the same time Joe waved his hand in the air for silence again.

". . . and I know you've already met her, but I'd still like to formally introduce her to you. The most lovely lady in the room, my wife—"

The color drained from her face. Betrayal tasted like ash

147

in her mouth. Having failed to win her by talking, he had announced this in front of all of them, her parents and his boss and friends, knowing that she would never deliberately be able to humiliate him, that as much as she wanted to walk out, to storm out, to deny—

"Come on up here, Bronwyn!"

She walked stiffly through the crowd, felt Joe's arm swing around her like a vise, smiled, and watched dozens of champagne glasses raised to her and Joe and his job and their marriage.

By one all the guests had left and the last of the caterers were at the door. Bronwyn was helping carry out the things from the kitchen, and when that was done she went back to look for Joe. Flushed, he was still drinking champagne, his long legs stretched out as he relaxed in the couch in the living room. He lurched up to a standing position when he saw her, giving her a beaming smile that was a little loose from all the champagne he'd had. "You were the most beautiful woman in the whole place, Bron," he slurred lazily. "Don't you think the party went terrific?"

She looked at him, and then turned to get her wrap. She wished for anger, but all she felt was hurt, and a kind of contempt for herself that she'd allowed herself to be manipulated. He had the job he wanted. She was happy for him. Any other feelings of guilt or obligation had died. "I'm going home."

"It's blowing like hell outside, darling," he protested. "We can stay here."

"No. You can. In fact, you'd better. You know you've had too much to drink to make a two-hour drive."

"Well, I can sure as hell drive you home. That's only twenty minutes." He smiled, beaming, again, stretching lazily.

"Joe, you just made it hard on yourself," she couldn't

148

resist saying sadly. "You're going to have to take it all back—about our getting together again. We're not. We never were."

"Yes, darling." She could see the wheels in his mind. Agree, cope with her tomorrow. As he had tonight. Out-maneuver, cut, and run.

She stopped trying. The ride home was silent, and, for her, unnerving. The wind had set up a steady nerve-tingling howl that penetrated even inside the car, and then it would stop suddenly, creating an eerie silence out of nowhere. At times the car seemed to be weaving, but at least luckily there was no one else on the road and his speed was not excessive. She hadn't realized exactly how much he had had to drink until she saw him behind the wheel of the car; her mind had been on getting home, ensuring that she was not stranded at the beach house with him.

"I need a glass of water," he said thickly when they got to her door. "My throat is so damned dry."

He tripped on the way into the house. Before he was through the door Gypsy had wakened from the front yard and come hurling through the night in an automatic bee-line of growling at Joe.

"Stop it," Bronwyn told her tightly, and the dog, unused to such a furious tone from Bronwyn, curled closer behind her.

"I'm going to kill that dog," Joe muttered.

"She's just trying to defend me."

Bronwyn watched Joe drink the water, then watched the glass slip from his hands and crash in a thousand slivers on the floor. All she could think of was that she couldn't believe she was actually going to have to put him up. She cleaned up the mess while he apologized over and over, until she thought her ears would close themselves off. He always drank his share at a party, but she had

149

never seen him this inebriated. The water seemed to have shot the alcohol directly to his bloodstream.

When she went back to the living room, she picked up his suit coat from the floor and draped it around a chair. Joe was standing, weaving, by the glass windows, looking out. "You'd better sleep in the bedroom," she said curtly.

He turned with a glaze in his eyes. "Is that supposed to mean anything interesting?"

"Oh, for God's sake." She was not amused. "If you sleep on the couch, it's with Gypsy. I'm not putting her out tonight in this weather. It's your choice."

"Sure, honey."

When the door was closed to the bedroom, Bronwyn remembered belatedly that she was still wearing her party clothes. She slipped off her shoes, went into the bathroom to brush her hair free from its spray and style, scrubbed off the layer of makeup, and slipped out of her stockings. She was totally exhausted. The gold raw silk would have to do as a nightgown, because she had no intention of going into the bedroom, or, for that matter, undressing any further with Joe in the house.

When she came back out to the living room and started switching off lights, Gypsy had some protesting to do over the evening of neglect. Bronwyn sat on the couch, leaning over to put both her arms around the dog, petting and stroking her affectionately. "I feel as though someone kicked me—hard," she whispered to the dog. "It's just the point of it, you see. It's not even that in certain ways he can be a very good man, and perhaps he even honestly believes that he needs me in his way. But I won't live like that anymore, Gypsy. I lived like that all my life, with people playing those kind of manipulative games. Do you understand?"

Slowly the dog lapped a tongue on her hand, trying her best to show love and support, snuggling closer with a husky little whimper. With a sigh Bronwyn adjusted the couch cushions so she would have a pillow and drew a thin cotton blanket over her. If she had to know that all her debts were paid to Joe, she did now. But the feeling was not of relief or satisfaction; it was a restless, unhappy sadness. The wind outside had totally stopped, but there was a pressure in the night air she could feel inside herself, an atmosphere filled with threat and tension.

She was wakened at an impossibly early hour by a steady pounding at the door. Disoriented by finding herself on the couch in the dark room, she half stumbled when her bare toe struck a table leg, and finally made her way to the door. Austin stepped in impatiently, dressed in old jeans and a hooded sweat shirt, his hair blowing furiously across his forehead by a wind that continued to howl until she closed the door. "You're beginning to make a habit of this," she said sleepily, referring to the last time he'd come so early in the morning. She smiled, and then chuckled at her own sheer delight at seeing him. "God, I'm glad to see you. I have so much I want to talk to you about."

He threaded both hands through her hair, raising her face up to his for a brisk kiss. "I've been trying to reach you for over an hour. Evidently your telephone is off the hook, Bronwyn. There's a hell of a storm brewing, hurricane material headed this way. I got Caro back just in time to get her out of here again, and then it suddenly occurred to me that you might actually be so foolish as to try and stay here."

His sweet, mocking tone dropped abruptly. She was looking directly up into his face, but finally she half turned, her eyes following where his seemed focused, several feet beyond her. She saw a man's suit jacket draped on the chair, a man's tie curled on the floor. He was taking in the slinky gold dress when she turned her eyes back to him. "You'd *both* better get out of the area," he said curtly, and turned away.

"Austin!" She grabbed at his arm, horrified at the sudden harsh pain etched across his features, feeling like splintering inside. "Wait a minute—"

"Honey, I've never judged you before, and I'm not now. All I'm thinking about is this storm, and that you'd better get that little butt of yours in gear and get moving. Get a radio on. Have you got a radio?"

"It's not what you think," she said desperately.

He pulled her fingers from his arm and dropped them as if they were hot. From a sound sleep she was suddenly remarkably close to hysteria, her tousled hair framing a stark white face, her huge brown eyes pleading with him. "Joe was drunk. I couldn't let him drive. I—"

"I told you before, Joe's your affair," he snapped curtly. "More power to you if you can make it together. It's nothing to me, Bronwyn. A good time had by all and no hard feelings. Now, put yourself back together, and I'd get that phone back on the hook before the lines are down. I wouldn't stay in the area more than a few more hours, not with the wind speeds they're forecasting—"

"Austin! Damn you! Listen for just a . . ."

He turned away and started walking. She took two steps after him and stopped. There was Mary and Carroll in the car, smiling and waving at her, and all she could see was the set of his shoulders as he walked away from her, as rigid as steel and as ungiving. He wasn't going to listen. And he wasn't going to believe her. Anguish wrenched through her as she went back into the house and closed the door against the screaming wind.

Gone. He was gone. Really gone, she knew that, left with that cold-blooded "a good time had by all and no hard feelings." His pride talking, or was that really how he'd felt all along? Just an interlude of sex and smiles?

Something thick sat in her throat. With trembling

fingers she pushed back her heavy mane of hair, icy fingers rubbing at her hot temples. She stood for several silent minutes, her thoughts wild and chaotic and her heart pounding out a beat of pain. Only then did she notice that outside her balcony the sky was as black as night, that the sky and the ocean blended indistinguishably on the horizon, both inky swirls of constant motion.

CHAPTER FOURTEEN

Bronwyn knocked once sharply on the bedroom door and then simply let herself in. Joe was sprawled on his back in his underwear, half covered by the sheet, and she noticed the phone receiver knocked to the side, when he had evidently flung an arm during the night. He still had those innocent and boyish features in sleep, very much the all-American, she thought bitterly.

"Joe, wake up!" She crossed to the side of the bed to replace the phone receiver. "Wake up!" She leaned over and nudged at his shoulder. "Come on, Joe. You've got to get out of here!"

He finally peeked out at her from beneath heavy-lidded eyes. "Come here, Bron," he said huskily.

His tone was strange. With a frown Bronwyn stepped back and turned, pushing open the shuttered closet doors to rummage for her clothes. "There's quite a storm coming. If you don't want to be stranded, you'd better get a move on," she said curtly.

Bracing a pillow behind his head, he said smoothly, "Maybe I like the idea of being stranded with you for a few days."

Her fingers stilled on the clothes in the drawer, and then she pulled out a short red T-shirt and slammed it. Not really noticing what else she chose, she grabbed a brushed cotton pair of pants, underwear . . .

"You don't like that idea, Bronwyn? You don't like the

idea of the two of us stranded alone here together for a few days?"

There was something odd in his voice. She turned to look at him, her mind still filled with Austin and the look on his face when he'd seen Joe's striped tie on the floor. "I'm not in a very funny frame of mind this morning. If you wouldn't mind—"

"But maybe I just would mind, Bronwyn."

He had had too much to drink last night, and had obviously not woken up in a pleasant mood. The blond hair was tousled boyishly, but his eyes were rimmed and heavy, a man's eyes at their coldest. She felt a menace of a kind. Not that she couldn't handle it, but that she felt like screaming for having to make the effort. "I want you out of here," she said coldly. "I don't know why you did it last night, Joe. I don't know why you called me your wife in front of everyone, and I don't know why you told me you needed help with your boss, when you had the promotion in hand. You had to know. I don't know what you were trying to prove—"

"Maybe I just wanted you to be my wife again, Bronwyn. And maybe I thought that when you saw how happy your parents were, it would make a difference. And don't think it didn't make a difference to the job, Bron. I didn't totally lie. When you weren't even trying, I thought a little push—"

"You thought if you put me on the spot that I'd have to give in? That I wouldn't have the courage to back down?" At the look in his eyes she knew that was true, and she shook her head, running a hand through her hair distractedly. "The worst of it is that I would have given in a few months ago," she said sadly. "Joe, I feel no love. I don't know how to put it any plainer than that. I wish you luck; I wish you the best; I wish you a woman in your life, if that's what you want. But that's all I feel."

She turned, the bulk of clothes in her arms, to go into

the bathroom. "It's that man, isn't it, Bronwyn?" Joe said gratingly from behind her. He lurched up from the bed and started walking toward her. "You think it didn't tear me apart when I saw Steele in your house that morning?"

"It's you and me that doesn't work," she said flatly. "It has nothing to do with anyone or anything else."

"The hell it doesn't!" Fingers suddenly grasped at her upper arms to swing her to face him. "I saw how it was, with your hair a mess and that look still in your eyes. I may have come because your father asked me to, but when I saw you looking like that, and thought about you sharing someone else's bed—"

"You're hurting me!" Frightened, her fingers clenched on his, trying to loosen the hold on her arms. He half shook her and she glared up into a stranger's eyes. "Stop it!"

"You never let loose with me, did you, Bronwyn? But, then, I started with the virgin—and how I coveted being the first with you! I thought I had to be so careful . . ."

"Joe—"

His lips fastened on hers, his teeth grating against her lips, drawing blood. Her flinch of revulsion seemed to make him all the more furious; his one hand clenched tightly in her hair as the other groped for her breast.

The next thing she knew she was tumbling backward, her temple colliding with the closet door. Gypsy was snarling between them and Joe was trying to get up from his knees, a terrified look on his face as the snarling mass of 140 pounds launched herself at him. *"Call him off!"* She would have, but she was stunned and shaking and there was bile in her throat that would not pass. In horror she saw Gypsy's teeth sink into Joe's leg and heard Joe's yelp of pain.

"Gypsy! Down! *Down!*" she screamed. The dog didn't even turn, too intent on defending her mistress against a man she had hated from the first moment she'd seen him. *"Gypsy!"* Bronwyn shouted again, stumbling forward to try to grab the dog.

Before she could stop him, Joe had reached from behind him for the heavy ceramic lamp on her bedside table and brought it crashing down on the dog's head. Gypsy gave one frantic yelp of pain, and then lurched and crashed to the floor.

The silence that followed was broken only by Joe's heavy breathing and his sudden frantic look at Bronwyn.

Her lips were parted, her eyes glazed as she stared at the suddenly still dog. On hands and knees she crawled to touch Gypsy's silky head.

"Look, Bronwyn, I didn't mean . . . For God's sake, the dog could have killed me! You couldn't have expected me to sit there and just take that!" He lowered his voice deliberately, backing away from her when she looked at him. "Bronwyn, God, I'm sorry—"

"Just get dressed and get out."

"Listen—"

Joe," she said, very quietly, "get out of my life. I don't want to see you again. I don't want to hear from you again. Just leave me completely alone!"

"Look." He hesitated. "I can't just leave you like this. If you tell me what you want me to do with the dog . . . Look, Bronwyn, I never meant to—"

A kind of numbness seemed to seep through her, everything very still inside except for a strange throbbing in her temples. "I'm not accusing you of anything," she said calmly. "I'm not sure what I would have done if a dog that size would have attacked me. I'm not blaming you. She . . . didn't obey." When he moved a few steps closer her eyes suddenly blazed. "Don't touch her. I'll take care of her. All I want you to do is get out of here."

He snatched up his clothes and backed away. In a moment she heard the bathroom door close and she closed her eyes. This was not happening to her. Austin hadn't left; Joe hadn't attacked her and her dog, her lovely Gypsy. . . .

Within ten minutes she heard the sound of the back door closing, and knew he was gone. She opened her eyes again, staring at the heap of still warm black fur. There was blood on the dog's neck. As far as Bronwyn could tell, the dog was totally still and there was no question . . . She touched the dog's head again, but her hands were shaking so badly that she could detect no movement. And her head was throbbing so badly that she couldn't think.

She got up finally, and managed to get out of the wretched gold silk dress. She drew on the T-shirt and cotton pants, such a blur of tears in her eyes that she felt dizzy, the simple task of dressing monumental. She didn't know what to do. She desperately wanted Austin. Austin was somewhere driving his daughter and Mary to safety from the storm, and, regardless, Austin was now out of reach for all time. So of course it must be that she didn't want him. She'd managed alone by herself for a very long time and she didn't want anyone.

She stared for long moments at the dog, aching, her arms nestled beneath her chest as if she could hold herself. Her sole companionship for so many months, all those quiet months until her life had gone upside down when Austin had come into it. Gypsy would have defended her with her life; Bronwyn knew that's all the dog had thought she was doing, why she hadn't listened to the commands. Just as she knew why Gypsy had had the instinct to never like Joe.

Desperately she wanted to put Austin from her mind, and just as tenaciously a vision of his face was lodged there. She had to think. She had to do something with Gypsy, for one thing, but the dog was too heavy for her to move. Irrationally she didn't want the dog moved anyway; she wanted to go out of the room and come back and find her alive and perky and demanding attention. Woodenly she went into the bathroom, came back with a damp cloth, and knelt beside the dog, gently blotting at the blood matted in Gypsy's fur. Then, realizing how futile that was if the dog were dead, she simply whirled, a feeling of desperation exploding inside of her. She dropped the cloth and ran.

Actually, she walked. Slowly and then faster, a pace set that hurt her lungs, that pulled and tugged at her calves, that increased the pounding in her temples. A feeling of numbness seemed to settle within her, so that the only thing she was aware of was the physical pain, and she kept on walking until she could no longer.

Breathing heavily, she sank to her knees in the sand, for the first time aware of the world around her. Her ocean had gone insane. The tide should have been low on the beach and, instead, was a filthy muddy froth spitting up ten feet of spray only yards from her. There was no air. The wind was hurling everything in the sky but air—fistfuls of sand, debris, twigs, driftwood. The sky was as low as a ceiling, a moving mass of intensely ominous clouds, swirling like oil in water at an incredible speed. The entire world was a yellowish charcoal—air, ocean, land.

The landscape was lonely and angry, exactly as she felt. She drew up her knees and buried her head in them, a chill despair creeping through that numbness. Joe's face flashed in her mind. *My wife,* he'd said with that brilliant smile, in front of so many, the brilliant smile so false. The look of her Gypsy, so helplessly still, those velvet brown eyes closed. God, Austin. *No hard feelings.* He would never believe her. Now it seemed that he'd never really cared.

She would get a grip on herself in a moment, but not yet. It wasn't there yet. At the moment she felt like she was dying inside, just like the world all around her.

After more than an hour every muscle started to cramp

and her stomach protested with nausea from having no food but nerves for too long. Still, it wasn't until she felt the first stinging pellets of rain that she actually lifted her head. She'd been so wrapped up in her own emotional turmoil that she hadn't seen how rapidly the weather had changed all around her.

Even just lifting her head, she was all but assaulted by a blinding stinging wind mixed with knifelike rain, a brawling world where she could barely see a few feet ahead of her. She started to stumble to her feet and found the force and fury of the wind something she could barely push against without falling down. Exactly where she was or where the house was she did not know. She could see nothing, and the ocean was rapidly approaching her, the spray striking her in freezing salty splatters when, bewildered, she half turned. Something struck her shoulder, and she startled again. A small piece of driftwood, but the force of it had frightened her, and she suddenly felt real fear.

Sheltering her face and hands as best she could, she crouched, half bent over, to start back toward the house, trying to lean farther toward the land side to get her bearings. The sand and hail stung like someone physically attacking her, and her motions were like a drunkard's, weaving to maintain balance against the force of the storm. Fear started to insinuate itself into her bloodstream like a slow-moving drug, like the urge to simply curl up like a child and pray it would pass over her. A thousand storms she'd seen in her life, but never anything like this, never where she'd felt alone in a universe gone insane.

Aching, she brushed her hair back, desperate to see. The sand attacked her face instantly, as if waiting for that vulnerable skin to show. She half turned away with a choked sob, half falling as she tried to make her way backward, then sideways. The green brush on the dune beside her was bent completely flat; the sand swirled in

160

long eddies, shifting as she tried to move. It was impossible; she seemed to have already been walking for hours and could not even be sure she was closer to home than when she'd started. The brush all looked alike, what little she could actually see of it. There were no houses close to hers, so she simply had no way of knowing where she was. If she could climb the dune, perhaps, find at least enough shelter to see, but the wind kept up its high-pitched screaming. Between the shrill wind and the attacking ocean she couldn't think, and terror began to take over until she was clawing at the sand to climb the dune, tears streaming from her eyes without even being aware of them.

Every limb ached so; her hair knotted into an impossible tangle, snarling across her face. It was even hard to breathe, the damp rank air seemed devoid of life-giving oxygen. At last she made it to the brush, so physically exhausted that she sank down helplessly. Even in that half hour since she'd started moving, the storm seemed to have doubled in intensity. She was soaked to the skin and still could not recognize where she was. All of it started to overwhelm her: the fury of the hail, the wind, the rain. Desperately she covered her head with her hands.

Then she felt those hands pulled up, then her body moved and thrust painfully close to a hard wall of shiny yellow slicker. Terror-filled eyes met Austin's, only for an instant before another rain slicker was being thrown over her head. There were no words—she was too exhausted to try, and Austin wasted no energy when it was at a premium. The shock at seeing him simply registered, but the overwhelming sense of relief blotted out the momentary surprise.

He gripped her tightly around the waist, and all but pushed her face to shelter in his chest, bearing a good portion of her weight as they started out. She put both arms around his waist and simply hung on, closing her eyes against the wind and sand, willing her feet to move as he directed her. Their heads bent and their bodies half crouched low against the screaming lash of needle-sharp wind and hail and salt. It seemed endless, that stumbling, torturous walk, and he would not let go; she had no breath left. . . .

She was barely aware that they'd approached the lee side of the house; her eyes did not open until Austin loosed his punishing grip on her. When he opened the door, it smashed wide and he practically shoved her inside as he turned to battle it closed again. Weakly she took a few steps forward and then collapsed on the carpet, dripping and shaking, not caring. Exhaustion blended with the simplest, most basic gratitude at the relative silence, the absence of the bite and sound of the wind. Her heart was still pounding, not seeming to know that finally it did not have to work so hard.

Finally she gathered the strength to look up. Austin was leaning back against the doorway, his hair dripping wet and his chest heaving as hers was, yet his eyes bored into hers like ice-cold steel. When he spoke, his tone was savage. "When I get my strength back, I'm going to beat the goddamn hell out of you, Bronwyn."

CHAPTER FIFTEEN

Bronwyn nervously touched a damp tongue to her dry lips. "I've been in storms before. Maybe inland, not on the coast, but I . . ." she started raggedly. "I've never seen anything like that. I didn't know . . . It seemed to get worse all at once."

"You could have been killed out there, don't you know that? I don't care what happened with him; no one's worth that, Bronwyn. What the hell is the matter with you?"

She didn't know what he was talking about. "I was . . . upset."

"And that he *left* you in this—never mind. There isn't time, and I just don't give a damn. Get up." He strode forward and jerked her up to her feet. "By some miracle the lines are still up—for now. I can guarantee that won't be for long. *Move.* Turn the faucets on in the tub to fill it up; start filling up every container you have with water. Get coffee going and fill thermoses if you've got them. And if you've got any way to get at least one round of hot food and keep it warm, do it. And get out of those clothes." At her shocked look for his clipped commands he said furiously, "*Now!* I don't give a hoot in hell how exhausted you are. I'm going out to lock shutters on what few windows you've got protection for, then I'll be back. Start thinking: Where are the matches, candles, flashlights. A transistor radio—"

The urge to fall apart fled abruptly when he slammed

the door and left the house. She felt it again, the surge to live he brought with him, the no-nonsense realities that mattered. The rest of the last twenty-four hours didn't matter, not now, not yet.

She hurried first to the tub to start the water, then shrugged off the bulky dripping rain slicker, barely aware she was still shivering violently. Leaving the faucet on, she hurried to the kitchen, set a huge pot of hot water to boil for coffee, and then started filling pots and bowls and pitchers, anything she had that would hold water. Dragging a chair from the dining room table, she stepped up to reach the cupboards above the refrigerator, bringing down two chafing dishes and a kerosene lantern she really never thought she'd have any use for.

Then she got the box of candles for the chafing dishes, and gathered the decorative ones she had scattered around the cottage. Almost too late she raced back to the tub and flicked off the faucets; it was full. Back in the kitchen she found a single huge thermos that she started filling with the boiling water. And then the lights went out.

For the middle of the day it was impossibly dark, an impossibly lonely dark. Her blood stopped racing, and an ominous chill shivered through her that only lessened when she heard the angry howl of the wind again. The door had opened; Austin was back and safe.

She struck one of the candles and set it on the table, opened the cupboard, and brought out two mugs, spooning liberal amounts of instant coffee into each. Her herbal teas—it didn't seem the time. She heard Austin shrugging out of the rain slicker as she poured the boiling water, then lifted his cup, preparing to hand it to him when he came into the room.

"I told you to change clothes."

"Yes. I will." His voice was still volatile. She looked away once he'd taken his coffee, and bent down to reach into the refrigerator for the pot of soup she'd made a few days before. By the light of the candle she poured it into the chafing dish, then lit another candle and set it beneath. His list of orders; they seemed to be done then, and she stole a look at him.

He was a devil with his shaggy wet hair and brooding eyes, his skin stretched taut over angular bones in that flickering light. The dark shirt and pants set off his dark skin, set off that image of brooding male power and attraction that had first drawn her. "Flashlight?" he asked curtly.

"In the drawer by the sink." She motioned. "But I haven't any extra batteries I'm afraid. There's a kerosene lantern and it's full—"

"No camp stove or—"

She shook her head. She had no way of cooking anything without electricity.

"We'll keep the refrigerator closed as much as possible. In a few hours we could transfer lunch meats or cheese to the freezer; we'll have at least a day that way before there's risk of spoilage. You'll lose the uncooked meats and freezer foods, but if we've got canned goods, we're in no trouble anyway. Two days, at most three—we could really make it on water if we had to."

Her jaw dropped. "I—that long, do you think?"

"At worst forty-eight hours for this kind of storm. I said three days because the minute it's over there still won't be instant power, or roads we can travel on, or food available at the corner grocery store." He paused, at last taking a long sip of the coffee, his eyes meeting hers over the top of the cup. "Get out of those wet clothes."

"I will," she repeated vaguely. His mind seemed to go a thousand times faster than hers. She was still absorbing the idea of having to listen to that wind for two days; he had already established their nutritional survival and was on how the power shortage would affect grocery stores a century from now. "I—Carroll?"

"And Mary—they're with my parents. Dad met us half-way when I called him, and inland they wouldn't normally be bothered by a coastal storm. Dad will handle it anyway if Matilda shifts gears."

"Matilda?"

"That's her name, brown eyes. The hurricane."

The unexpected use of the nickname warmed her like heated brandy in her stomach, made her suddenly breathe freely again. It was the first hint that he was losing his rage. She wanted desperately to ask him why he had come back at all, but he wasn't making much of a secret of the fact that he'd rather be anywhere else than here with her, and she didn't want to make that worse. It was all she could do to hide a knife-sharp pain when she looked at him. That *a good time had by all* echoed relentlessly. She lowered her eyes to the coffee cup. "Austin, do you think the house . . . ?"

"We'll move what we can of your furniture up and off the floor shortly. As far as living, your spare room is the safest. Everyplace else has sliding glass doors. I know they're made to meet standards these days, but we're not going to be the ones to put them to the test. I told you before about those loose shingles. There isn't a prayer they'll hold. The leak'll start probably between your bath and bedroom. If the breakwall gives, you could have water in—not drowning water, just a mess," he qualified impatiently at her look of dismay, then added a little less brusquely, "If you have a chess set we'll survive very well. Not caviar-and-champagne well, but there is nothing to worry about. What problems there'll be we'll fix, some sooner, some later. Now, you're shaking like a leaf, if you don't know it, so—"

"I can't go in there," she interrupted. He'd stated the disasters but reduced them all to handleable; *those* kinds of truths she could handle.

"Pardon?"

166

"I can't go into the bedroom to get my clothes. I can't. In a few more minutes . . ." She shook her head wildly. "Gypsy. I just need a few more minutes."

"Bronwyn?" He took a step closer and she frantically waved him away. As coldly as he'd been treating her, it would just be better if they didn't touch.

With a frown he turned on his heel, grabbed up the candle, and left the room. He was gone a long time. She heard a crash and clatter and cringed, knowing he must merely be dealing with the broken lamp, but thinking of Joe crashing that lamp down . . . Her eyes closed, aching at the thought of even a moment of pain for the dog who had loved her so much. Just too much had happened, and the cold neutrality in Austin's face made him seem like a stranger. She felt both raw and exhausted and horribly vulnerable.

"Honey?" Austin was back in the doorway, bracing both arms against the doorjamb as he stared piercingly at her. "She's unconscious, brown eyes, not dead. Is that what you thought?"

She turned slowly, her voice quavering helplessly. "Are you sure?"

"I'm sure she's alive. And that no bones are broken, although I can't promise you . . ." He ran his fingers roughly through his hair and sighed. "I don't understand. How on earth . . . ?" Even by candlelight he could see the welling of tears in her eyes just as she could see the deepening frown on his forehead. "It just doesn't matter, not now," he said swiftly. "I'll go in and get you some clothes if you want—"

"No." She set her cup down. "It's all right then. I . . ." Her chin set more firmly; mentally she forced the tears to dry. "You need clothes as well. I have a man's T-shirt I sometimes sleep in, but for pants, I—"

"I'll dry. I was covered where you weren't," he said roughly. "And one thing we don't need to cope with is pneumonia. So . . .." He handed her the candle and she took it.

Once inside her bedroom, she closed the door, took a long look at the dog, and rapidly stripped off her damp clothes. Her plants in the corner of the room set off crazy shadows on the wall—a flickering mouse, a butterfly, a strange mask. The wind was like a muffled keening just beyond the closed curtains, a lonely, empty sound. Draping the wet clothes on hangers to dry, Bronwyn drew out her warmest caftan and pulled it over her head, covering herself from her neck to her toes. Her flesh was so cold that she craved the snuggled softness of velour, its warmth.

She drew her brush through her tangled hair as she curled down to a kneeling position by her dog, the candle placed carefully on the carpet beside her. Her fingers, no longer trembling, found the heartbeat, so elusive before. Gently she probed through the heavy mat of fur. The gash was clean, dark, and swollen at the base of her neck. Gypsy did not so much as stir. Bronwyn sat back on her heels, staring helplessly at her, and then, in a moment, stood up.

Austin said nothing as she crossed to the kitchen. He had an end table in his hands he was carting to the spare room. She saw that he was in the process of moving furniture, protecting it should water come in. She should be helping, she thought fleetingly. It was her house; she was the one who had gotten him into this.

She set a candle beneath the spare chafing dish and rummaged in the near dark of the back cupboard for a small bag. The roots she took out had to be mashed, and everything was annoyingly difficult without proper light. Finally she had a cupful of ingredients over the flame, while she searched for linens.

"I don't think I've ever smelled anything worse."

She started, pivoting on one foot to see Austin suddenly leaning over the counter, watching her.

"Should I label you witch, Bronwyn? What the devil are you up to now?"

Impersonal curiosity, easy humor. All the heat was gone from his eyes, as if they'd never treated each other in any other way. She lowered her eyes back to the countertop. "It's for Gypsy," she said quietly.

"Obviously another one of your herbs?"

"Comfrey again," she confirmed. "I used the leaves for my shoulder, but for that gash of hers the thing is boiled roots, applied directly. The purpose is to reduce the swelling, relieve the pain. . . ." In spite of herself her voice caught. *Why can't I just tell you about Joe? Why won't you ask?*

"Bronwyn. That dog is feeling no pain. And if she's unconscious, she's better let be."

She nodded. "I know that. Rationally. But this can't possibly hurt her, and—" She shook her head, carefully spooning the gummy mixture on the clean white linen to cool. "There is just no way I'm going to let that dog lie there."

"Bronwyn, she is not hurting," Austin promised her softly.

"But I am." Carefully she lifted the cooling mixture to take it back to the bedroom. Austin soundlessly carried the candle to light her way.

It took a bit longer for the mixture to cool, longer for Bronwyn to cleanse the cut and snip the fur surrounding it. Her caftan fell awkwardly around her as she tried to work on her knees; finally and carefully she smoothed the sticky mixture onto the sore and loosely covered it with a cloth.

She knelt back on her heels, aware that Gypsy still hadn't so much as moved. Doing something, nevertheless, made her feel infinitely better. Admitting to herself that she was hurting lessened some of the tension within as well. She hurt for Gypsy. A thousand times more than that she hurt because she loved the elusive man behind her to distraction, and there seemed to be a wall between them, an inpenetrable wall that kept growing.

She stood up, almost weaving with exhaustion. Austin caught at her arm to steady her. "Go into the spare room and lie down. You've had enough to handle today."

She shook her head. "I would rather watch her—"

"I'll keep an eye on the dog, Bronwyn. Go on. Now."

"I—" He was right. She just couldn't think anymore. She poured some of their precious water into a bowl to cleanse her hands of the herb salve, and then all but stumbled into the spare room. He had been working. Her couch cushions were set up on the floor like a bed; the cot unearthed from the closet for a second. Everything was piled differently. None of that mattered. She tossed a pillow on the cushions and sank down on them, curling up with a blanket over her. For the first time in years, it seemed, she was finally, really warm. Just ten minutes of rest she craved, and then she was going to have that talk with him, going to have to find a way to break that wall. But she needed ten minutes . . .

Something cool and gentle brushed her forehead, and Bronwyn stirred reluctantly. Though still groggy, she saw a pair of sky-blue eyes just above her, full of the sensual warmth and promise that she'd just been dreaming of. There was a ripple of frown that didn't quite belong between the brows. Sleepily she reached up with her fingertips to erase that frown, her palm lingering on the curve of his cheek.

Austin closed his eyes at the touch of her hand, and then opened them. With a smothered guttural sound from his throat his lips came down on hers, his arms wrapping around the soft voluminous velour surrounding her. Her lips parted responsively, her skin luxuriating in his possessive hold. Like a slow-motion dream his palm cupped the velour to her breast, then kneaded down her side to her hips. She stretched out next to him, arching her body seductively, her hands slowly trailing down his back to his hips, just as he had done to hers.

She was halfway between a deep sleep and wide awake, a state of feeling languidly, sensually hypnotized. In the shelter of his arms the wind seemed only an erotic whisper; the flickering candle flamed over the contours of his face and its shadows, the deep shadows of his eyes as his face again bent down to hers. He looked the ruthless pirate, but the tongue that plundered inside the soft darkness of her mouth was gentle, soft, evocative.

Her fingers splayed, tightened on the rough denim of his jeans, the primitive female in her drawing in her mate. In response, the pressure of his mouth increased, a fierce possessive pressure that incited suddenly more than a tender touch of tongues, more than dream-filled sensual play. She was awake now, and she wanted him. She wanted the walls down and the truths told and all the realities he'd taught her. Not cloth, but flesh. Not the veneer of behavior, but the core of emotion. Her hands slipped beneath his dark sweat shirt. His flesh was so warm in her hands, so vibrant; her fingertips teased up the curly-haired surface of his chest, resting on the smooth orbs of his nipples. They hardened, just as her own were hardening, and beneath her palms she could feel his heart pounding.

Restlessly he shifted next to her, his lips pressing a fierce trail of fire down her neck. His fingers groped to find an opening in the neckline of the caftan that simply wasn't there. Impatiently his hand trailed back down, tugging at the loose soft folds as his mouth came back to hers, hungry, so helplessly hungry, a sensual wildness that ached within him for release. Still his hands battled with the long loose material, and she felt like laughing in sheer joy. That

171

crazy caftan! "Oh, Austin, I knew you didn't believe I'd ever slept with Joe——"

Abruptly his head rose from hers; his hand stilled. Groping for breath, he stared at her, and then suddenly wrenched up and away. So rapidly his eyes changed from sensually loving to glacierlike, staring at her distractedly as he raked a hand through his hair. "Damn it! I only came in here because I thought you were ill! You were asleep for nearly four hours!"

In a moment he was gone, the door slammed shut behind him. Raggedly she pushed her hands through her tousled hair and sat up, pain coursing through her at his swift rejection of her. But her body flowed with life whenever he came near it. And he really did believe she'd slept with Joe. Confusion and anguish washed over her pale features as she stared at the flickering candle. Maybe he wanted to believe that. When it came down to it, he'd never spoken of love or commitment; it was all in her, in her heart. So he physically wanted her—that was not news. A man could physically want any woman and not want a commitment. More than once he'd indicated that Joe had first rights; not once had he verbally objected to her seeing Joe in any way. The opposite had been true.

So what do I do? she thought in despair. *What am I supposed to do for the next two days, pretend I don't care?* The only thing she was certain of was that Austin would never believe that last night had been innocent between Joe and herself.

She thought of her pride, of his. Forty-eight hours was a very long time. Long enough to wage a war and still keep her pride? Long enough, she decided desperately, to try.

CHAPTER SIXTEEN

It was such a crazy feast. The lamplight was flicking up shadows in the corners of the spare room, up the sides of dusty paintings and easels, chairs stacked high, flashlights and first aid equipment, and whatever other emergency supplies were haphazardly laid on the table. Austin was sitting on the couch cushions, and their dining table was a low coffee table, with plastic knives and forks for their cutlery.

Still, it was a feast Bronwyn kept bringing in from the kitchen. A cheese fondue with bread bits, vegetable soup, raw peas and broccoli, marinated tomatoes and mushrooms, slices of cold meatloaf and ham, a whipped-cream cake, relishes . . . "God in heaven, we couldn't possibly eat all this," Austin chided her.

She shook her head. "It will spoil if we don't." She sat down at right angles to him on the cot. It had been all day since she'd had more than a bite of bread, and she didn't hesitate to fill her plate. Austin followed more slowly, a half smile on his face as he watched her hungrily devour the food. A half smile that did not quite reach his eyes. He'd taken only a bite or two before he laid down his fork. "You look more like yourself after that rest."

She glanced up. "I should hope so. Four hours!" She speared a bite of dried bread and dipped it into the melted cheese.

173

"So don't you think it's time you told me what happened to the dog?"

She swallowed, then took a sip of wine, not looking at him.

"Gypsy attacked Joe. The lamp—it was the only thing there was at hand to stop her." Her tone was as neutral as his. She picked up another forkful of food, and his hand closed on her wrist.

"Wait a minute. What sort of sense is that supposed to make? Why the hell should she attack your ex-husband?"

The hand on her wrist let go, and she swallowed the food that had suddenly turned dry. "She never liked him."

"That doesn't answer my question," Austin grated.

"What question?"

His still features tightened in exasperation. "Bronwyn, that dog. When she was in the water with Caro, the child was all but clawing the dog's eyes out to get free in a panic. Caro was a total stranger, yet the dog just let her continue to mawl and scratch. Don't tell me that dog has a temper problem, because it just won't wash."

Bronwyn nodded neutrally. "Up until now I never saw the least sign of temperament in Gypsy," she agreed. "For that matter, I can think of no occasion, except with Joe, when she didn't obey a command from me."

"So why did she attack him?"

She sighed. "Because he touched me, Austin. Is there anything else you want to know?" she asked bluntly. For a moment she just stared at him, desperate to find some sign that he actually cared. But rather than concern or jealousy or anger, there was steel in his expression, a hardness accented by the lamplight.

"You'll have to do something with the dog when you go back with him then," he grated out crisply.

She took a breath. "Is that what you want to hear, Austin? That I'm going back with him?"

"I think we'll both do well to change the subject," he said curtly.

In a moment she got up to bring back a dusty bottle of wine from the kitchen. Not being much of a drinker, she had every hope that a single glass would dull her senses, and she wanted her senses dulled. She poured out two and handed Austin his.

"To the storm?"

"To the storm," she agreed, meeting his eyes. The darkness had enlarged his pupils so that his eyes appeared like black mirrors; she could see her own reflection in them, the dark hair and dark caftan, the soft play of lamplight on her face. She finished her dinner quickly, merely filling her stomach, no longer tasting the food. Strength, she told herself. "Do you mind if I ask you something?" she said idly when he pushed aside his plate and leaned back against the wall, his wineglass in his hand.

"Shoot."

"Was the heroine in your story your ex-wife, Austin?"

He stretched out his long legs, a raised eyebrow communicating very clearly that his ex-wife was as appreciated a subject as Joe was. "The book was fiction," he said roughly.

She chased the last of the peas around her plate. "In the story I thought the hero blamed himself for the husband's death. That he believed he was responsible because he'd slept with the wife."

Austin set down his wineglass with a little clatter. "Bronwyn," he said harshly, "I can think of a dozen other things we could talk about besides this. It was all a hell of a long time ago. More than seven years."

She nodded, her lashes shadowing her cheeks as she looked down.

"When I met Renee, I'd been nearly a year in the wilds of Alaska without a woman. I fell, like ninepins. Is that what you want to know? That I feel guilty for her husband's death, because I let her sway me when I shouldn't have? You're damned right. I did and I do."

"And you vowed never again to become involved between a husband and wife," she said softly. "No matter what the evidence that their marriage might have totally disintegrated."

She could see the muscle in his cheek working when she stood up. "I'll just clear this up," she said quietly. Getting under his skin was exactly what she wanted to do, but it suddenly didn't feel like that. There was more tension in the room than air. What could be worse than being stranded with a woman who was hanging on, when you'd all but told her she was free to go?

But Bronwyn was confused. The signals when he touched her were so different from when he spoke. And she couldn't just let it drop without being absolutely positive of how he felt. She couldn't just let the only man she'd really loved up and walk out of her life.

She spent a long time in the kitchen. The normally fastidious room was an incredible disaster area—the counters were filled with water containers, it was gloomily dark, and sand had crept in. She could feel it on her bare feet on the floor. The wind kept howling, and the freezer had to be emptied, the dishes managed somehow with a minimum of water. Humidity had seeped through the closed-up house, and when she was done with the chores she was also broiling. The rich dark caftan was perfect when she'd come in freezing from the storm; now the material clung heavily, the weight of her hair clinging damply at the nape.

She took a candle and locked herself for a few minutes in the bedroom, peeling off the caftan. She pulled a cool ivory shift over her head, picked up a brush for her hair and a handful of hairpins. Off her neck she felt cooler, the loose careless knot feminine and cloudy around her face. To cool herself she sprinkled perfume liberally on her

176

throat and shoulders, just a light scent. Beneath the loose garment she wore nothing but bikini briefs. Because it was hot, she told herself, as she knelt to check on the dog again.

The gash seemed less inflamed, and she believed that Gypsy stirred a little when she stroked her. "You and I know why I'm dressed like this, don't we, sweetheart?" she whispered to the dog. Austin had first kissed her in that shift. She didn't know how to get through his wall without risking the slap in the face she was afraid was coming. But she had to keep trying.

Austin poured the wine while she dealt the cards. It was eleven at night, though neither of them was particularly aware of it. Time hardly mattered. The darkness, the wind, and the heat kept building up regardless of the hour.

"Seven-card stud, low in the hole with an option. Pay a nickel on a one-eyed jack and ante of one," Bronwyn directed smoothly. Her stack of pennies at the moment equaled Austin's. Joe used to refuse to play with her because she always won. Austin was another story. For an hour she'd had the momentum because he'd obviously not expected a woman to be a decent poker player, but she had no illusions in the long run as to who controlled the cards.

"Up yours two, lady." He tossed a pair of pennies in the pot. "While you were sleeping this afternoon, I took another look through your drawings, Bronwyn. Didn't you say something about doing something with them?"

"Match your two and raise a penny. Stop distracting me, Austin," she chided him absently, tossing back an errant strand of hair.

He was sitting without a shirt. All right. It was hot. But the candlelight gleamed like apricot fire on the smooth skin of his muscled shoulders, and his chest hair curled. She reminded herself that she'd always hated chest hair on a man. She liked smooth civilized skin, like Joe's, only

177

every time she glanced up at Austin she remembered exactly the sultry feel of that black hair on the soft flesh of her bare breasts.

"That's two hands in a row, brown eyes. You're slipping."

She took a breath. "Is it my deal?"

He nodded.

"Fine." She shuffled and started dealing. "Five-card draw. Threes, fours, and fives wild."

"I beg your pardon?" The slash of a smile reflected the distinctly feminine turn to the game.

"If I deal, I call the game," she said defensively.

"Whatever you say."

She won that hand, lost his deal, then won hers. "It's no good, the painting," she said finally.

"Why not? What do you mean?" He half frowned, shuffling the cards, giving her a curious glance.

"At least as an interior designer I could hold my own, support myself."

"You don't need to support yourself."

"On paper, thanks to my grandmother's trust. But that's just spoiled, Austin. People have been taking care of me all of my life. It's no good doing something just because I want to do it. Joe saw it. Joe all but cut the project to ribbons when I thought it meant so much to me."

His jaw tightened at the word *Joe*. "Bronwyn." He laid the cards down, folding his arms on the table to stare at her. "I'm not an art critic. I don't think I need to tell you your work's damned good, but maybe that's not the point. You've spent months, so don't tell me it's not important to you."

"I didn't say that."

"Then what the hell are you talking about?"

She took a sip of wine, not meeting his eyes. "I'm talk-

178

ing about doing what I have to do, not necessarily what I want to do."

"That doesn't make a penny of sense. You don't just give up something you've put your whole heart into. So you're lucky you don't have to starve while you suffer through the opening gambits; that doesn't mean you couldn't make it in art in the long run. How the hell are you going to know if you don't give it a chance?"

The lies were already on her lips, something she'd been preparing for hours. She poured herself a second glass of wine, liking the claret hue through the candlelight. "You're the one who convinced me otherwise," she said quietly. "Not so much about the painting, but about Joe. You're the one who said I should do what I have to do." She took a sip of the wine. "And then I read your story. A marriage can break up, but there are certain ties from it that can't be broken, just simple things—years of hanging two toothbrushes together, if that's what it comes down to. An obligation, a responsibility, a kind of caring even if it isn't loving. Even if it isn't loving at all. Even if it isn't what you want."

"Bronwyn . . ."

She shook her head. "You opted for love, Austin, and it's torn you up ever since, with your Renee. If I were to ask you for advice, isn't that what you would tell me—that love isn't worth much, really, not when it's at someone else's expense? That doing what you want doesn't pay? Every time I've mentioned Joe or you've seen him with me, isn't that really what you've been trying to tell me? That I don't have the right to walk away from my obligations to Joe, regardless of what I feel or felt for you, or any other man, if it came to that?"

"Bronwyn." He set down his glass with a clatter that splashed a single drop of wine by the candle. Lurching up, he dug his hands in his pockets and turned from her.

"That isn't what I told you. I told you to make very sure how you felt—"

"No," she said quietly. "I think if you'd wanted to know my feelings, you would have asked me. If you'd wanted to voice your own, you would have told me. You communicated in other ways, Austin. When you choose love, there are certain risks—risks of loss, risks of hurting other people, affecting their lives. It's not worth it, is it, Austin?"

He turned, his jaw so tightly locked that the muscle in his cheek was working, his eyes flaring brightness to hers. "That's never what I said."

"Then *ask* me," she said in a low voice.

Like a man holding tight to his emotions he stalked from the room without looking at her. She could feel the color drain from her face, and then slowly she gathered up the cards to put them away and stood up. Her heart was beating too fast; now that he was out of the room her hands were trembling. She'd tried. Three times. When he asked about the dog, she'd implied Joe's touch, hoping for a sign of jealousy. She'd hinted at dinner that he saw too much of his own life in hers and Joe's. And last she'd tried to hint at the love she felt, at a love he could feel if he were willing to take the chance. Again he'd shut her out. She didn't have any more pennies to bet with.

She took the pins from her hair and set them in a little pile on the table, then brushed out the long strands until her hair was silky and smooth. She took off the shift, and slipped between the cool sheets, tucking them modestly around her.

A long time later she heard him come in, this time very quietly. She heard the woosh of the candle being extinguished, smelling that instant of smoke; heard his jeans unsnap and the sound of material as it was pulled off in the darkness. The wind seemed to pick up its eerie whine when the lights were off, and shed a restlessness that made

180

it difficult to lay absolutely still. But she did, aware when he crouched over her, aware when his hand smoothed the sheet yet closer to her neck, aware when his palm rested just a second longer than necessary on the silk curtain of her hair. Then he moved to the day bed, and the two of them lay a long time in the darkness, both pretending to be asleep, willing the storm to end.

Bronwyn kept her eyes tightly closed, sealing the tears within, praying she could breathe around that desperate, hopeless lump in her throat.

CHAPTER SEVENTEEN

"Bronwyn?" Gently the hand shook at her shoulder, and sleepy and startled she turned to Austin's voice. For a moment she was disoriented, the room so strange, the darkness still total. "It's the eye of the storm, brown eyes. Come out."

The sheet slipped down to her waist as she perched up to a sitting position. A pair of creamy breasts glowed by the light of the lantern he held, partially shielded by her dark cloud of hair. She was looking at Austin, still trying to stir from the deep exhausted sleep of the night. "You mean we can go outside," she asked softly, distractedly. He wore jeans, no shirt, his hair disheveled and dark, and in that odd light she saw huge shadows beneath his eyes. She knew he hadn't slept. "What time is it?"

"Five."

She stood up then, and the cool air on her skin made her aware finally that she was uncovered. Automatically she groped for the sheet, but not before he had slammed down the lantern and taken two steps forward. The sheet was wrenched from her hands and draped all around her, tucked tightly around her neck like a noose. In a moment it was done and he was striding out ahead of her, but not before she had a glimpse of his face, not before she'd seen the stark emotion in his eyes and felt the roughness of his fingers. He was not immune. He might have her believe that principles blinded him to any other emotions, but he was not immune.

Cautiously she followed him through the dark hall and living room. He was standing at the sliding glass doors, waiting for her, and as she came forward he opened them. For the first time she was aware there was no sound of the wind. She stepped out on the cement terrace behind him, and simply looked.

It was neither night nor day. The world was gray, and the stillness was eerie. The tide was as high as her break-wall, the surf pounding a gray spit of rubble onto her flattened grass. A century plant had survived the winds; all of her flowers and other plants had been uprooted. There was a chair in the yard. She'd never seen it before. Driftwood was piled in one corner of the house as if some-one had stacked it there. Above them the sky was furious-ly shifting yellow-gray clouds in a kaleidoscope of patterns, but totally without sound.

The only sound seemed to be that devil surf, pounding in that ominous, ceaseless rhythm. All that bleakness and destruction—and the surf kept pounding. She raised stricken eyes to Austin.

"Bronwyn," he said softly. "There's nothing to be frightened of." She shook her head. "It'll be rough for a few more hours, but then it will start tapering off. You'll go back to sleep—"

She shook her head again. "I can't go back in there."

He shook his head back at her, smiling as he stepped forward. His hands laced around her neck under the dark curtain of her hair and he pulled her gently to him, resting his chin on the top of her head as they both stared out at the bleakness. "Aren't you silly," he whispered teasingly, and then softer, "The whole world can just go ahead and come tumbling down, Bronwyn. Don't you know I still wouldn't let anything happen to you?"

His arms felt like her haven, her cheek resting in the

warm curve of his shoulder, her breasts cradled to the firm wall of his chest. She kept one hand on the sheet to keep it in place, but the other curled around the bare skin of his back. The trembling, she couldn't help it, she couldn't stop.

"Bronwyn." He tilted her chin up to look at her, his expression concerned, grave. That changed quickly as awareness added a certain cloudiness to his eyes. "There's nothing to be afraid of," he repeated.

But there was. Smooth and warm, his lips touched hers, and mindlessly her own parted, she, on tiptoe, desperately reaching for reassurance, for the man who was Austin. His arms tightened around her, his fingers splaying in the weight of her hair as the pressure of his mouth increased, a hungry, desperate pressure that seemed to explode in the man. She forgot the storm, responding to him with her soul, breathing in his flavor and passion and strength. Restlessly her hands kneaded into his back, cradling him closer, trailing up his spine to curl in the hair at the nape of his neck, holding him to her.

His lips left hers to press deep, almost biting kisses in her neck, then as smooth as petals his mouth trailed back up her neck to the line of her jaw and her cheek. "God, I love you," he whispered. "I need you; I need your softness, the woman you are. I don't care . . ."

The wind, like a spirit, suddenly picked up to hurl a salty spray at them. Austin, looking softly down at her, suddenly raised his eyes. Already there was the bite of the sand and the low, keening pitch of wind again, as if the eye of the storm had never been. And Bronwyn could see the tightening of Austin's jaw as he took control of his emotions, not looking at her again as he grabbed for her sheet-covered shoulder and pushed her into the house. Even in those few seconds their skin took on the dampness of the air and he closed the door, standing there for a moment before closing the drapes on nature's devastation.

She stood, staring at him, the sensual emotions he'd wrought not faded yet, something else becoming stronger.

Avoiding her eyes, he half turned. "You'd better get back and get some sleep."

Something burst inside. He was going to pretend that he'd said nothing. Tortured brown eyes stared at him, and then suddenly she felt the heavy nudge of fur on her bare calves and looked down. "Gypsy!" She knelt to the sleepy-eyed dog who whimpered as Bronwyn tried to soothe her. Momentarily distracted, Bronwyn got up again to bring back one of the precious bowls of water from the kitchen. Gypsy lapped nearly a full bowl and then lurched drunkenly back to Bronwyn's bedroom. As Bronwyn followed her, the dog was already closing her eyes again as she settled heavily on the floor.

"She'll be all right soon," Austin said quietly from behind her.

She rose from her knees, not looking at him, adrenaline suddenly pumping in her veins. She was relieved at Gypsy's waking . . . There was joy, but so much stronger than that were other emotions at the moment. She walked past Austin and into the living room, waiting for him to come back in.

"Do you want something to drink?" he asked when he did come in.

"I want to know if you meant what you said." She was in the center of the room, a fallen flap of sheet baring one shoulder as she stood with her hands on her hips.

"What are you talking about?"

"Do you love me?"

He sighed, staying where he was in the shadowed doorway. "Bronwyn, you're tired. And outside you were frightened—"

"Do you or don't you?" she demanded.

"I love you like hell. Is that what you wanted to hear?" he shot back tightly.

It was like an explosion inside, knowing it, hearing him say it. "Then why didn't you ask me? Ask me if I slept with Joe? Ask me if he matters to me!" Mindless and furious, she felt like the storm outside, a desperate anger that had no outlet. She reached for a pillow on the floor and pelted it at him. There was another. "Damn it! I don't care about your Renee! I'm not Renee! Maybe I was a total fool. Maybe it took me too damn long to figure out that I really didn't have any kind of obligations to him, but you're a bastard if you think I could have slept with him after sleeping with you!" The tiny ivory elephant she'd kept on the table crashed on the wall near his head, barely missing him though he didn't move.

"How *dare* you think I would do that?" He hadn't moved one chair to the other room. Its top cushion was propelled and then the bottom. She lurched back up, frantically seeking something else.

"God in heaven. You pick up that lamp and I'll tan your hide!"

"You think it's nothing that I slept with you—no commitments, no promises, no . . . nothing!" The lamp clattered back in place. She grabbed a pillow again, hurling it. "Maybe you do see it as nothing. Maybe that's the way you live—jumping from bed to bed. I don't know. I don't care. I'll tell you this. It's an absolutely stupid way to live, like asking someone to kick you in the teeth!"

He ducked beneath the next pillow, came out from underneath it to snatch at her palm before it landed on his cheek. His mouth seared down on hers, firm and silencing. "I almost think you're trying to tell me you love me, brown eyes."

"How could you not know?" She was shaking from anger and frustration and hurt, from his turning away from her so many times, as if he just didn't give a damn. But his lips told her otherwise, a rich, teasing pleading with hers to calm, to give in to his. His body cushioned

186

her shaking, and like velvet he was slowly smoothing his hands up and down her bare back as the sheet slipped in a tangled mess to the floor. When his lips pressed on hers, her neck arched back, her hair swaying behind her as she desperately reached around his neck to hold on. "I love you," he murmured when he finally lifted his head from hers, his eyes dark and emotive, so grave.

A blur of tears rainbowed in front of her eyes. "Austin, why didn't you say it?"

"Why didn't I push you? You think I couldn't see that you'd suffered, Bronwyn, that you were just making your way back into life? You left your husband at a time when your world was falling apart. Who was to say what you would feel about him when you surfaced to real life again? You had to find out for yourself. I couldn't push you, Bronwyn—not the way I love you. Can't you see that?"

She heard his words. More importantly she saw the look in his eyes, a depth of loving so intense that it calmed the last of her frantic rush of emotions. Only one emotion remained. The one that matched his. She reached up to run soft fingertips on both sides of his face.

"When I thought he'd spent the night with you . . ."

She reached up swiftly to kiss the ragged sound from his lips. "You came back."

"I came back," he echoed. "When I met my father, and Mary and Carroll were taking care of . . . I already knew I wasn't going with them. I kept seeing you in my mind, the way you looked when I walked in. I kept seeing you in that gold dress, the dress you must have been wearing the night before, Bronwyn, and if you'd actually been . . . with him, you'd hardly have still been wearing a party dress. It didn't make sense. The only thing that made sense was getting back here. And when I saw you in that storm, I thought he'd hurt you, that he'd left you . . ."

187

She understood. Lovingly she reached for him, wanting to erase those visions from his eyes, to replace them with ones that mattered. His skin, so warm and vibrant against hers, stirred a welling of love inside her so full and joyous that she felt drowned in it. With the splash of rain and gray hurling wind all around them, the man above her seemed golden, holding her eyes with his own, blocking out everything but the sheer loving look of him. Intense, her man, a man who stole every moment of living from love, who took with such sensitivity . . . she wasn't as strong as he was, not yet. But she could imagine nothing she couldn't do with him at her side, an entire lifetime of possibilities.

He brought her alive again, with the touch of his hands and the touch of his lips and the touch of the spirit of the man. They sank to the smooth cool sheets, an embrace of fire, of storm, of celebration. When she closed her eyes she had the vision of rainbows.

Candlelight Ecstasy Romances™